I0631162

Lady Adelaide Cadogan

Drawing-room plays selected and adapted from the French

Lady Adelaide Cadogan

Drawing-room plays selected and adapted from the French

ISBN/EAN: 9783337278861

Printed in Europe, USA, Canada, Australia, Japan

Cover: Foto ©Andreas Hilbeck / pixelio.de

More available books at **www.hansebooks.com**

DRAWING-ROOM PLAYS

SELECTED AND ADAPTED FROM THE FRENCH

BY

LADY ADELAIDE CADOGAN

ILLUSTRATED BY E. L. SHUTE

Dedicated by permission

TO

HER ROYAL HIGHNESS PRINCESS CHRISTIAN OF SCHLESWIG-HOLSTEIN,

PRINCESS OF GREAT BRITAIN AND IRELAND

LONDON

SAMPSON LOW, MARSTON, SEARLE AND RIVINGTON

Limited

St. Dunstan's House

FETTER LANE, FLEET STREET, E.C.

1888

This little book is intended to meet a want often felt—especially at Christmas-time—of short plays, unobjectionable in tone, easy to act, and requiring no elaborate costume or scenery. The following lines were written for the Authoress by a friend to whom she had expressed her regret that the language required was necessarily 'of the period.'

To the Reader.

My task has been a hard one—to express
French wit and sparkle in an English dress.
Forgive me, Reader, if your cultured taste
Think language 'of the period' misplaced :
'Pals,' 'beastly,' 'rotten,' 'bosh,' 'confound it,' 'hang,'
Are, I admit, 'quite too too awful' slang,
And if you disapprove of 'won't' and 'can't,'
To the poor solecisms pardon grant.
We know, of course, professors do not teach
These little idioms of our Saxon speech,
But in the grown-up world, that larger school,
Such forms are not exceptions, but the rule :
So please remember that in '88
We English neither live, nor talk, in state,
And if, with this in mind, you like the plays,
My best reward will be—your honest praise.

CONTENTS.

CAUGHT AT LAST.

Characters.

MR. ANTONIO ALDERSON .   *Barrister.*
MRS. WILLOUGHBY .   *Young Widow.*

SCENE :—*First floor room in country house. Window at back.*

MRS. WILLOUGHBY. [*Enters hastily, holding a basket of work, which she puts down on a table, and shuts the door energetically. Speaking through the door to some one outside.*] Jane, call Thomas, send to the stables, anywhere, everywhere, for the coachman ; get a mousetrap. Shake everything in the dining-room, rummage in the passage, but— living or dead—that mouse must be found. Above all, don't let any one open this door, even if I'm to be shut up for a week with nothing to eat or drink—do you hear, Jane ? If the mouse gets in here I shall go mad. [*Sits down.*] Now to think that such a creature should be seen in my house—my house of all places, and a perfectly new one into the bargain ; I shall have to live in a balloon. . . There I was, quietly sitting by the window with my work; my feet were frozen, so I put them into my muff-bag . . . and, oh, horror ! a brute of a mouse darts out, actually scampering over my feet. Ugh ! I screamed like a maniac. I had just presence of mind to seize my basket, and then ran for my life, across the passage and dining-room, and here I am [*looks at herself in a little glass*], and in what a state, to be sure ! I look like a mad woman, and at any moment that Mr. Alderson may be here. He's

B

been worrying me for the last three months with letters, and hitherto I've declined to see him. . . But he has somehow contrived to curry favour with Lady Scott, an old aunt whose heiress I am. It seems that he manages her affairs; and under pretence of consulting me about important business connected with my inheritance, he asked for this interview, which I naturally couldn't refuse. . . It's a dodge, no doubt, to force me to see him, but I shall tell him frankly, once for all, that I don't mean to marry again—not him at any rate. Oh! I've no patience with the man; besides, his persistent correspondence might compromise me. Well, he'll find me in a nice temper, if he finds me at all, for now I come to think of it, how can I receive him if he comes before they've caught that horrid little beast; as I daren't open the door.

A Voice.   Mrs. Willoughby, m'm.

Mrs. W.   Have you caught it?

Voice.   No, m'm; a gentleman.

Mrs. W.   Caught a gentleman?

Voice.   No, mum, there's a gentleman who insists on seeing you.

Mrs. W. [*aside*].   It only wanted this to finish me. [*Aloud*] Mr. . . Alderson, of course?

Voice.   Here's his card, m'm.

Mrs. W. [*running to the door*].   Don't open the door, Thomas; don't open the door, poke it underneath. [*Picks up the card and reads it*].   Yes, Mr. Alderson, I can't send him away after making the appointment, especially as he has come all the way from London. . . . Then I shall feel safer with somebody near me, and in talking I may forget the little brute.   Thomas [*speaking through the door*], go and explain to Mr. Alderson that the bolt of this door is broken, that I've sent for the locksmith, and ask him if he'll mind going round by the garden and coming in—by—the—window. [*Goes to the window*]. And, Thomas, if Mr. Alderson consents, bring the little ladder from the greenhouse.   At any rate, the mouse can't get in that way.

A VOICE. Very well, mum.

MRS. W. [*goes to the fireplace and arranges her hair before the glass over the mantlepiece*]. Oh dear! what a state my hair's in; I really must tidy myself, for I haven't a doubt that Mr. Alderson will be too delighted to scale my window. He'll think he's acting Romeo at our first interview [*goes to the window*]. Here he comes, just turning the corner. He's not bad-looking; but he seems astonished, as well he may, at my odd proposal. He's rather stout, however, and he looks aghast at the ladder. Hum, if I ever did mean to marry again, it might as well be this same Mr. Alderson as any other, for one hears nothing but good of him. He has the character of being honourable, clever, and a thorough gentleman, though rather eccentric, I suppose on account of his foreign blood; his mother was an Italian or something. However, I have quite decided to keep my liberty; and so I shall give him clearly to understand. [*Opening the window*] A thousand pardons, Mr. Alderson. . .

ALDERSON [*speaking from below*]. Let me assure you, my dear madam, that there is no occasion for excuses. I am only too happy. [*Aside to the gardener*] The ladder is pretty firm, is it not, my man? Yes? Thanks [*aloud*], too happy, as I repeat, to come into your house for the first time by the way one so often wishes others to go out.

Mrs. W.   Shall I give you a hand ? [*She holds her hand out to him*].

ALDERSON.   A good omen, indeed, for one who comes expressly to . . .

Mrs. W.   Ah ! take care.

ALDERSON [*putting his leg over the window*].   Thanks. [*Entering, they bow.*]   Let me first express my gratitude for your kindness in receiving me in this charmingly unconventional fashion.

Mrs. W.   You will easily believe that I'm terribly put out at having to receive you in this manner, but it's the fault of the mou—, of the locksmith I should say, and your time being so much occupied—and—and—coming from such a distance, I thought it best to offer you . . . [*pointing to the window*].

ALDERSON.   The ladder. [*Wipes his forehead, aside*] It's worse than the underground.

Mrs. W.   I fear the exertion of climbing up has exhausted you . . . won't you sit down ? [*drawing forward an armchair*].

ALDERSON.   Yes, it was rather a climb ; but [*grandiloquently*] to conquer without peril, would be to triumph without glory ! [*sits down*].

Mrs. W. [*sitting down*].   I hope you bring me a good account of my dear old aunt, Lady Scott. What a charming woman she is—such good company.

ALDERSON.   May I remark that her niece, in that respect, takes after her ?

Mrs. W.   Oh, dear no. I've no right to take after her. She was only my husband's aunt.

ALDERSON.   Ah ! yes, I remember ; your excellent husband used to speak of her.

Mrs. W.   You knew my husband ?

ALDERSON.   Yes, poor man [*movement of Mrs. W.*], well, poor is not the word, perhaps ; one uses it conventionally. I knew him first at school, and later on we were called to the bar together. For the last few years I have been so absorbed in the duties of my profession, that we have scarcely ever met. Indeed, you can hardly realize how a barrister's time is taken up, especially when one has had—like myself —some degree of success, but for the last three months I have cared for no success but in one cause, and look for no favourable decision but from one judge.

Mrs. W. Indeed, Mr. Alderson. Who is the one judge whose decision is so all-important ?

Alderson. Mrs. Willoughby, it is *you !* For the last three months I have sighed for *you* as the thirsty stag pants for the limpid stream ; I love you with an adoration immense, ferocious, melancholy, as, in short, we with Spanish blood in our veins know how to love.

Mrs. W. Spanish or English, you express your sentiments in singularly plain language, and I must say that . . .

Alderson. In the glowing South, dearest Mrs. Willoughby, nothing daunts us. We jump from resolve to execution in a single bound. To reach the woman we love, we stem the roaring torrent ; traverse the burning forest ; aye, grapple with the wild beast in his den.

Mrs. W. I am certain you would show all the ardour of the most chivalrous hidalgo, but it is not on me that such devotion should be wasted. My resolution is unchangeable, never to marry again !

Alderson. Never ?

Mrs. W. Never !

Alderson. Then you have given me my formal dismissal, and there is nothing left for me but to retire.

Mrs. W. But surely you are not going away until you have explained the important business which you mentioned as the reason for coming ?

Alderson [*with pompous decision*]. Indeed, Mrs. Willoughby, after the decided resolution you have just expressed, there remains nothing more to be said, as to the question on which we differ. . . . I have only therefore to regain the window by which I [*looks doubtfully at the window*] . . .

Mrs. W. [*absently*]. I beg your pardon, but don't you hear something scratching at the door ?

Alderson. The locksmith no doubt. . . . And I confess that I should prefer this door rather than the [*points to the window*].

Mrs. W. I do not think it's the locksmith. [*Aside*] Oh! if it was that horrible little beast again.

Alderson [*going to the door*]. Let me at least find out . . .

Mrs. W. [*running after him*]. No, no, quite unnecessary—I can ring. [*Aside*] Oh! I can't let him go—he is some sort of protection.

Alderson [*aside*]. What can be the matter with her ? [*Aloud*] You seem agitated . . .

Mrs. W. I ! Not the least in the world.

Alderson. Some unexpected affair no doubt. . . . If you had only told me sooner. . . . However, I will at once rid you of my company.

Mrs. W. No, no, pray stay. [*Aside*] His presence gives me courage.

Alderson. But, Mrs. Willoughby, I should grieve to disturb you, and though certainly that exit is not so convenient . . . [*Goes to the window.*] Good heavens ! the ladder has disappeared.

Mrs. W. [*Aside*]. What luck ! [*Aloud*] So you see you're my prisoner. [*Aside. Listening at the door.*] I hear the same scratching and the servants don't come. [*She pulls the bell hastily—the cord breaks*]. There, this is a pleasant fix.

Alderson. I am certain, dear madam, that something is amiss ; you are ill, perhaps ?

Mrs. W. [*impatiently*]. I never was better in my life.

A Voice. Did you ring, mum ?

Mrs. W. [*running to the door and speaking through the keyhole*].

Yes! and broke the bell-rope; are you all deaf? Well! have you caught it?

A VOICE. Yes, m'm. Jane saw the cat creep under the sofa, and then run away with his prey; and then he leaped with it right on to the roof of the greenhouse, where he can be seen now.

MRS. W. Why on earth didn't you come and tell me so at once? [*To* ALDERSON.] Just excuse me for one moment. [*Exit.*]

ALDERSON. What does all this mean? Rushing off to watch her cat perched on the roof; and the door which just now . . . on account of the locksmith . . . and yet which now. . . . I can't make it all out — what an eccentric house. I arrive an hour ago—the door is de- nied me. I was told to climb up to the win- dow by a ladder, so unconventional a pro- ceeding that I con- sidered myself landed, . . . and risked a pro- posal. [*Pause.*] Not at all! I am clearly

given to understand that I might just as well have stayed below.— Then, when about to retire in good form, I am stopped. I prepare for a fresh assault . . . am again repulsed with loss! Then I feel there is nothing to be done but to return by the way I came, when, lo and behold! the ladder has disappeared, and the door, which was said to be hermetically sealed, flies open! A curious house; it's all very curious—very cu— . . .

MRS. W. [*speaking outside the door*]. I tell you, Jane, that what he's holding in his paws is more like one of my balls of worsted than a

mou— . . . At any rate, I'll count how many balls there are left.
[*Enters quickly, carefully shutting the door, and takes up her basket.*] I
must apologize, Mr. Alderson, for leaving you so long. But . . . a
matter of the highest importance . . .

ALDERSON [*aside*]. Highest ? she must mean the roof ! [*Aloud*]
I only waited your return to present my respects and to renew my
sincere regrets for having disturbed you. [*He bows and goes towards the
door.*]

MRS. W. [*vehemently*]. No ! no ! I beg you not to open that
door. . . .

ALDERSON. But . . . surely . . . Mrs. Willoughby . . .

MRS. W. Pray stay here . . . I assure you I was much interested
in what you were telling me ; and while I'm . . arranging my work
. . . we could . . . have a little talk. . . . Do sit down. [MRS. W.
sits on the sofa, and points to a chair.]

ALDERSON. By all means. [ALDERSON *takes a chair.*]

MRS. W. [*counting her balls of wool, nervously*]. We were
speaking of wild beasts, were not we ? Had you ever to struggle for
your life with one ? [*Aside*] Five, six, seven.

ALDERSON. It happened to me . . . once.

MRS. W. [*continuing to count*]. Then pray tell me all about it.
[*Aside*] Nine, ten, eleven.

ALDERSON. With the greatest pleasure. It was in the month of
September, at Seville.

MRS. W. At Seville ? Wild beasts at . . . Seville ?

ALDERSON. The environs were no doubt infested with bears and
tigers ; but that was in the time of the Romans. At the period of
which I speak, the same animals were to be found . . . in cages ! . . .
A magnificent menagerie was established in the public square, to which
enormous crowds flocked. One evening, as the public were eagerly
contemplating the delightful spectacle of a boa constrictor devouring a
poor little rabbit, an awful bellowing was heard, and turning round I

saw a gigantic lioness that had escaped from its keeper, advancing majestically towards me. The terrified crowd had already left the galleries, and were struggling at the door. . . . I, alone, remained ; and waited with a firm front, the onslaught of the terrible animal . . . armed with the umbrella which I now hold . . . when suddenly . . .

MRS. W. [*who has been listening to the recital while counting her balls of worsted, lets the basket fall, out of which the mouse escapes. She utters a piercing shriek and faints away*]. Ah ! there it is ! . . .

ALDERSON [*who, during his ·tale, armed with his umbrella, had turned away, leaps up, and falls into a defensive attitude*]. Ah ! the lioness ! ! [*turning round*] Heavens ! she has fainted. My narrative was too realistic for her nerves. . . . Mrs. Willoughby ! Mrs. Willoughby ! [*he slaps her hands*]. . . . If even it had been true . . . but as it is . . . imagine my feelings ! What it is to be a born orator ! Do try to recover. She doesn't stir ! What's to be done ? The bell [*he looks at the bell-rope*]. Broken ! At any rate I shall find some water in the dining-room. [*Exit.*]

MRS. W. [*recovering*]. Where am I ? Oh ! I remember [*looks round*]. Mr. Alderson gone ! What will become of me ? This little brute is sure to get among my petticoats [*gets up and passes to the left*]. Oh ! I see something moving [*she jumps up on a chair near the window*]. I'm safe here, at any rate.

[*Re-enter ALDERSON, carrying a bottle of water.*]

ALDERSON. I could only find this. [*He goes towards the sofa ; then sees Mrs. W. up on the chair.*] By heavens ! She must have gone mad.

MRS. W. Mr. Alderson !

ALDERSON. Yes, Mrs. Willoughby. [*He recoils.*]

MRS. W. Mr. Alderson. . . . You are brave !

ALDERSON. Certainly I am . . . [*clenching his umbrella*]. Most certainly—but . . .

MRS. W.   Having ·fought with a lioness, you cannot be afraid of anything ?

ALDERSON.   Assuredly not.   [*Aside*] Why the devil does she stay perched up on that chair ?

MRS. W.   Then, for heaven's sake, Mr. Alderson ; [*incoherently*] forgive me.   I am but a woman, and it is . . . more than I can stand. Kill it, Mr. Alderson, kill it, I beseech you ! . . .

ALDERSON.   Eh ?

MRS. W.   Ah ! I was certain it was only one of my balls of wool that he held in his paws.

ALDERSON.   His paws !   [*Aside*] She is out of her mind with terror.

MRS. W.   I saw it, Mr. Alderson.   I saw it with my own eyes.

ALDERSON [*aside*]. She saw it. . . .· There she had the advantage of me, for it's more than I did! [*Aloud*] Where did you see it?

MRS. W. Under this chair.

ALDERSON [*gives a jump; then stoops down and pokes with his umbrella*]. Under this chair? I see nothing.

MRS. W. I assure you I saw it hide itself there.

ALDERSON. But what . . . what did you see?

MRS. W. The mouse!

ALDERSON [*he turns pale and jumps on a chair at the other side of the window*]. Under this chair, you say?

MRS. W. Yes, a mouse—Mr. Alderson—a mouse.

ALDERSON. A mouse! Mrs. Willoughby [*he clasps his hands*]. I could live among crocodiles, I could eat with a leopard, I could sleep by a rhinoceros, but if there exists upon earth an animal which paralyzes me with terror, that animal is a . . . mouse. Call some one, dear madam—call the servants. . . .

MRS. W. But that's just what I can't do. The servants are at the other end of the house—they couldn't hear me—but you, Mr. Alderson, for pity's sake go and fetch somebody.

ALDERSON. If, dear Mrs. Willoughby, you were to offer me 10,000*l*. a year, or make me governor of the Bank of England . . . . it would be utterly impossible for me to . . . . move. I repeat to you that I am—paralyzed.

MRS. W. But we can't stay like this for ever. [*Turns anxiously to* ALDERSON, *who is looking at something.*] Do you see it?

ALDERSON. No, I do not see anything. But where, in heaven's name, did he come from?

MRS. W. Out of my work-basket, where he had been hidden. Ah! I see the curtain moving.

ALDERSON [*who had put one leg down, draws it up quickly*]. Which side, dear madam, which side? I beseech you, say nothing unless you are quite sure. · These shocks unnerve me. [*He drinks out of the bottle.*]

MRS. W. [*entreatingly*]. Listen to me, dear Mr. Alderson. You say that you . . . love me. You proposed to me just now. . . . Well! I swear to you that I'll marry you, if only you will rid me of this horrid little beast.

ALDERSON [*incoherent*]. By heavens, Mrs. Willoughby! you may believe me—on my soul I swear it . . . that above all things . . . and that my one object in life is . . . but I know myself too well . . . and if I were to touch that mouse, I should die on the spot, and you would have a corpse for your husband.

MRS. W. Still, Mr. Alderson, something must be done. I can't stand this position much longer. My back's nearly broken. If we could only get that door open, the servants might hear us.

ALDERSON. Happy thought. . . . I'll try with my umbrella. [*He pokes with his umbrella and succeeds in opening the door.*]

MRS. W. Well done. Now we must frighten the little wretch and try to make it go. [*Throws down her handkerchief.*]

ALDERSON. Failure number one. Now for another try. [*Opens his umbrella*]. Kish! kish!

MRS. W. Failure number two . . . [*She claps her hands.*]

ALDERSON. Wait one moment. I have an idea. [*Imitates a cat.*] Mieu, mieu. [*The mouse darts out and escapes.*]

MRS. W. There! Thank goodness it's gone. Shut the door quick.

ALDERSON [*vaulting down and slamming the door*]. And Buffon affirms that the instincts of animals never deceive them. That mouse mistook me for a cat! Natural history must be written afresh. [*Gives his hand to* MRS. W.]

MRS. W. Well! It was time we were rid of it! I'm perfectly exhausted. I fear you will have but a poor opinion of my courage. [*She comes forward and sits on the left.*]

ALDERSON.   And what can I say for myself, who, unable to over-come the repugnance with which that mouse inspired me, have thereby risked the failure of the dearest wish of my life—the possession of that hand—which you so generously offered me, and which . . .

MRS. W.   And which you did not know how to win! Pshaw! There's an end of it, and probably a very good thing for us both.

ALDERSON.   Then so it must be! For I have proved myself undeserving of such happiness.   But that which grieves me beyond measure is the knowledge that I leave you—believing me to be an arrant coward!

MRS. W.   Oh dear no.   I have a higher opinion of your courage than you credit me with; and if I could still doubt it, I'm sure you will give me a proof to the contrary.

ALDERSON.   In what manner, dear madam?   I swear . . . only prove me—command me.

MRS. W.   It's a very simple proof after all—only to go down by the same way you came up [*showing the window*], lest the mouse should get in by the door [*showing the door*].

ALDERSON.   Ah! the win-- . . . willing—ly [*gaily*]. You remember, I daresay, that they took away the ladder?

MRS. W.   Yes, yes.   I remember.

ALDERSON [*going towards the window*]. You remember? [*He measures the height with his eyes, makes as if he intended to spring, looks up, and sighs.*] Now for it . . . forgive me; one favour only I would ask. . . . Have you a spare room . . . unoccupied just now?

MRS. W.   Yes; there's the pink-room.   Why do you ask?

ALDERSON.   The pink-room. . . Oh! simply for information. . . . Thanks.   As I am certain to break one—if not two of my legs, it is a great consolation to be sure of a . . . domicile for a month or two.

MRS. W.   A month or two?

ALDERSON.   Or three! according to the nature of the fracture.   I would also venture to ask you to send for a surgeon as soon as possible. [*He feigns to put his leg over the window-sill.*]

Mrs. W.   Mr. Alderson, Mr. Alderson, I can't allow it!

Alderson.   Too late, dear Mrs. Willoughby.   I have sworn ; and we who boast descent from a Cortez, never draw back.   [*The same by-play.*]

Mrs. W. [*frightened, holding him by the tail of his coat.*]   But, Mr. Alderson, you *shall not* try it, I forbid you.

Alderson [*solemnly*].   Mrs. Willoughby. . . . If you were to go down upon your knees, you would *not* succeed in getting me to break my oath. . . Have the pink-room prepared.   It may not be for long, probably not more than a month or so.   [*Same by-play.*]

Mrs. W. [*getting more and more frightened.*] Stop! Stop! I absolve you from your oath . . .

ALDERSON. Out of the question, my dear lady. [*Aside*] Now for a bold invention! [*Aloud*] As you know, I am learned in the law, and the law declares that only as her husband can a man be thus absolved by a woman. That proud position you refuse me. . . . Farewell! . . .

Mrs. W. [*Aside*] . . . Caught! [*Aloud*] Well, then . . . since —it—must be . . . [*She puts out her hand.*]

ALDERSON. You accept me? Oh! joy unutterable. [*Kisses her hand.*]

VOICE [*outside*]. Mrs. Willoughby—mum; the little cat has caught the mouse. . . .

Mrs. W. It appears to me that the large ones are still more dexterous. [*Looking at* ALDERSON.]

ALDERSON [*clasping his hands and falling on his knees*]. How can I find words to express my rapturous happiness, my gratitude? what shall my first present to you be?

Mrs. W. The first one, let me see. . . . Oh! a mouse-trap!

CURTAIN.

EXCHANGE NO ROBBERY.

Characters.

CAPTAIN GEORGE LISTER.
LOUISA MAYNARD, *his Cousin.*

SCENE :—*A Garden in a Seminary for Young Ladies—a wall at the end—shrubs and bushes, under one of which is a bench.*

[LOUISA *runs in and throws herself on the bench. She wears a shady garden hat and holds in her hand a book from which she reads out sentences from time to time.*]

LOUISA [*reads*]. "Britain, however, was independent, and a great part of Gaul was conquered only a little later." [*She breaks off.*] What a mercy to think that I shall soon have done with this horrid place! It's rather hard to have been sent back to it after six blessed months of liberty, but my uncle said he couldn't leave me alone while he went on his tour of inspection. [*Resumes reading.*] "All the Roman legions displayed a Standard which had the figure of an eagle borne on the top of a spear." Oh! bother the Romans! [*throws book on ground*]. Why couldn't he have taken me with him? There's to be a shooting party at his place very soon ; I wonder if any of the men will turn, will turn into—admirers? that's the word Miss Wilcox uses instead of lovers in our history books! But what low form—I, who

C

set up for hating everything that isn't "prunes and prism"!   One gets
demoralized by the trash one hears talked, and yet it's rather hard on
the girls, for what can we talk about?   If we speak of other girls, it's
Missy; if we hint at the existence of a man, we're voted fast; or of
animals, we're called unfeminine, and indeed, as the donkey at Caris-
brook Castle is the only animal we come across,
it would be difficult to err in that line; and as
for sports, battledore and shuttlecock is about
the most thrill-
ing excitement
we have.   It's
a horribly mo-
notonous   life.
I wish something would happen
—anything.   [*At that instant a
note fastened to a stone is thrown
over the wall and falls at her feet.
She jumps up excitedly.*]   Here's
something anyhow, and it can't
have dropped from the clouds;
somebody must have thrown it—how
exciting [*She seizes the note and throws
the stone away, and begins to read, but stops
short.*]   It's not directed to me.   Ought I to
read it?   But then it's not directed to anybody, and how can one find out
who it's for without looking?. . . . If I leave it here, the gardener will be
sure to find it and take it to Miss Wilcox, and somebody may get into an
awful row.   After all, why shouldn't it be for me as well as for any one else
. . . so here goes.   "Dearest Mary" (not for me at any rate), but then
there are nine Marys here.   How can I help the right Mary unless
I . . . [*reads*] "Your father is still bent on marrying you to your

cousin ; but trust to me to find a way of escape, [oh !] If you will meet me this evening after your supper I'll explain my plan [ah !] and if you will but be true to yourself, all may yet be well. Be at the end of the garden at nine o'clock . . . P.S.—Whichever of the young ladies picks up this note is entreated to give it secretly to Mary—our united gratitude will be hers for life." . . . Ah ! now the murder's out. My only friend in this school is Mary Trevor, and she told me she was to marry her cousin ; she didn't seem enthusiastic at the prospect, cer-tainly . . . but . . . she said nothing about this other one [*pointing with her thumb over her shoulder*]. Now what ought I to do ? I heard that this cousin behaved beautifully about something connected with her father's affairs, and I know that Mary respects him, and lately, at any rate, she has seemed perfectly happy, so wouldn't it be a pity to upset her ? and after all this one [*again pointing over her shoulder*] may not be half so worthy of her. [*She twirls the note about in her hand.*] To think that I—the steady one—always lecturing the girls on the error of their ways . . . am holding in my hand a clandestine love-letter. I must say Mary is in luck ; two of them, and poor, poor me older, and already been out for six months, I've nothing to boast of, *nothing ;* indeed, for the matter of that, I've sounded the very depths of ignominy ; . . . *I've been refused !* . . . It's a fact ! My uncle proposed to his son, George Lister, to marry me . . . and George said he would rather be hanged ! I quite agree with him as to marrying, though I'd rather not be hanged as the alternative. Heigh ho ! how it takes me back to old days, when George and I were devoted to each other ; but those childish loves never turn into the right kind, and we haven't met since. It was rash, however, on his part, to refuse me without having seen me again ! Perhaps some day he'll repent in dust and ashes, and then what fun I shall have . . . I mean to lead him such a dance when I see him again ; but about this note, what shall I do ?

GEORGE [*looking over the wall*]. Here I am !

C 2

LOUISA [*turning round and uttering a faint cry of alarm*]. Oh dear, how you startled me.

GEORGE [*quite at his ease*]. [*Aside*] I'm blest if it isn't the wrong one. [*Aloud*] Oh! I'm so sorry, I'm afraid I frightened you.

LOUISA. Not exactly, but—

GEORGE [*astride on the wall*]. Beg pardon, but were you—that is—are you —you know what I mean—expecting some one ?

LOUISA [*with dignity*]. I expecting some one ? Certainly not. . . .

GEORGE. Then might I without being indiscreet . . . [*He jumps down and approaches her*].

LOUISA. Good heavens, what have you done ?

GEORGE. Scaled the wall—that's all. But do forgive me for coming like a burglar, I assure you I've the most peaceful intentions, and I think I see by your face that you guess them. Are you a friend of Miss Trevor's ?

LOUISA. A very great friend.

GEORGE. Oh, then of course she has given you a message for me— only why don't she come herself ? She's not ill, I hope ?

LOUISA. No, Mary is quite well.

GEORGE. Then do speak, my dear

Miss—? [*aside*] so awkward when a fellow don't know a girl's name [*aloud*] and put me out of my suspense. You saw the note.

LOUISA [*looking at him doubtfully*]. Y-e-s.

GEORGE. Then didn't you read the postscript?

LOUISA. Oh yes, I read it all . . .

GEORGE. Then, of course, if you're her friend you won't hesitate a moment. Slip it under her desk, or put it under her pillow, that's what all girls do for each other. Oh, do make haste! You don't know all that depends upon it . . . Poor Mary! I'll wait for you behind the wall, [*confidentially*] and one of these days you'll think of me, when some one you love scales this—same—wall. By-the-bye, don't forget to tell him of this particular spot; it's such an easy one. There now, I see you will give her the note, but . . . do make haste.

LOUISA [*hesitating*]. Perhaps I may . . . but it must be on one condition; you must tell me the whole truth and not conceal anything.

GEORGE. All right . . . you shall have the whole history from beginning to end; well, well, not quite the end yet . . . A year ago I came back from India, and at a garden party at Lady Smarthouse's I saw a young girl . . . she was eating strawberry cream . . . and as I was standing near, she asked me to get her some chocolate cakes. It was the eagerness with which she asked me for those chocolate cakes, and then for some iced lemonade, and then her intense enjoyment of them—that—first made me—

LOUISA [*interrupting him and laughing*]. In short you fell in love with her because she was greedy.

GEORGE [*laughing too*]. She looked so lovely; her little hands hardly able to grasp all the things she asked for; and then I hate the fashionable attenuated creatures who boast of living on air. . . I like jolly, healthy girls, who enjoy the good things of life and get fat upon them.

LOUISA [*laughing*]. Not a romantic beginning, I must say.

GEORGE. Oh, I was really in love, and afterwards I saw her constantly . . . I used to give her no end of bonbons ; she adores burnt almonds especially, and then . . .

LOUISA. Well ? . . .

GEORGE. Well then, you see we got to be great pals ; but I don't suppose we . . . should have thought much more of each other . . . only the other day . . . I'd been away for a bit . . . I heard of her father's smash, and that poor Mary was forced into marrying a cousin she hated. I heard that she was miserable . . . so . . . I rushed off here at once . . . to save her from a dreadful fate, poor little dear, and—By Jove, it's getting late.   Now do make haste.

LOUISA [*aside*]. He seems a quixotic kind of youth, and not a bad sort . . . I wonder if he means to go about disentangling all the engaged couples who don't care for each other ? he'll have his hands full at that rate.   [*Aloud*] One word more, in the first place what do you mean to say to Mary ?

GEORGE.   In the first place ? Why naturally . . . that I adore her.

LOUISA.   Next ?

GEORGE.   Next ? Why next I'll carry her off . . . of course.

LOUISA [*horrified*].   You propose to run away with Mary, and you expect me—to—

GEORGE [*interrupting her eagerly*]. To help us ? naturally—as you're her friend. I've arranged it all first-rate . . . I've got my pockets stuffed full of bonbons—to amuse her, poor little thing, till we get to London—then we go straight to a registrar's office . . .

LOUISA [*interrupting him aghast*]. You suppose that Mary would be married in a registrar's office, and that I would consent to— such a crime ?

GEORGE [*airily*]. No help for it ; as she's under age, we can't do the bann or licence business without her father's consent. Of course he'll give it when he knows we've been married the other way, and then we can go to church . . . oh dear, if you'll only get my note to her somehow . . . we've wasted such a lot of time already.

LOUISA [*aside*]. Flattering. I suppose he's very much in love, and can think of nobody else ; and yet he don't give me the idea of it . . . What on earth am I to do? if she does care for this man, who is evidently a good fellow, and if she hates the other one . . . which, however, I don't believe ; I suppose I ought to give her the option. [*Meditates.*] I'd better tell him the truth about Henry Danby— and then, if he still insists, I will give Mary the note, and she must decide. [*Turning to* GEORGE, *aloud*]   Do you know the rights of the case about Mary and her cousin ?

GEORGE.   Only the bare fact—that she hates him—and has got to marry him.

LOUISA.   About the hating I'm not so sure.   Colonel Trevor left the army, and dabbled in some sort of speculation, I suppose ; anyway, he lost every shilling, and but for this nephew, they would have been in the workhouse.   Henry had been in love with Mary for years, and only waited till he could settle in England to propose—but when this smash came he helped his uncle through, and never made a sign to her, so that she mightn't feel obliged to accept him out of mere gratitude . . . Wasn't it nice of him ? it only came out by accident. Of course Mary was touched, and I fancy she got to be fond of him. But, whether or no, . . . she couldn't throw him over now—I appeal to you—could she ?   And, supposing that she did care for you . . . would it be kind to tempt her ?   For, depend upon it, she would never be happy if she did—

GEORGE [*moved*].   Is this really true ?

LOUISA.   As gospel.

GEORGE.   Then you're right.   Mary's not the girl to throw over such a good fellow [*tears up the note*] ; and I wouldn't try to make her do it . . . But it's hard lines . . .

LOUISA.   I felt all the time that you weren't the man to urge her . . . It's very odd, but you put me in mind of a cousin of mine—who always began by doing the wrong thing, and always [*she laughs*] well . . . generally . . . ended in doing the right one! [*Aside, while* GEORGE *lounges about, and draws patterns with his stick on the gravel.*] I've been talking like Minerva.   I feel perfectly exhausted by my own wisdom.   Now I must have a good look at this—Lothario.   Till now I've been afraid, for he seemed a cross between Don Juan and a bandit, but now I like him.   [*Looks at him critically.*]   Very good-looking— thoroughly gentlemanlike ; and he reminds me of somebody . . . I can't think who. Now for another word of wisdom . . . and then the "something" that came to the rescue of my boredom—will vanish, at any rate as far as I'm concerned. [*Aloud*] Well, you'll have the reward promised by our copy-books to virtue, but as the gardener is sure to be here directly . . . please . . . you'd better go . . .

GEORGE. Where ?

LOUISA. Why, over the wall of course.

GEORGE [*preparing to get back over the wall*]. I wonder if virtue ever does bring its own reward ! I feel rather a fool ; and it seemed all so jolly and easy. [*Catching himself up.*] I mean, of course, that happiness seemed so near.

LOUISA [*demurely*]. The reward of a good conscience, you know.

GEORGE. Then I have only got to wish you—Good-bye ! Yes, one more favour . . . When Mary is married, mind you tell her that George Lister was faith—

LOUISA [*aside, making an exclamation that nearly betrays her*]. George Lister. Oh !

GEORGE. Eh ? . . .

LOUISA [*laughing*]. Oh ! it was nothing ; but I really must go now—Good-bye ! [*Goes out, hiding her laughter.*] [*Exit* LOUISA.]

GEORGE. Eugh ! I feel decidedly small ; and what an idiot I shall seem to the coachman and my servant—both sworn to secrecy. But it would have been a beastly shame to bowl over that good fellow if Mary had . . . I wonder if I shall be wretched, and all that ? I s'pose I'm in love with Mary ; and yet—I wish I'd found out the name of that other little girl. No ! not little—on the contrary—tall and slim . . . Well, her name can't matter to me—I only like small fat people . . . But there was something about her—and, thanks to her, I feel a model of virtue. It's a pity I can't see her again, for one doesn't live up to that form without some kind of help. She must have the highest admiration for my moral qualities, and perhaps if we meet later on . . . It's funny, how she puts me in mind of that cousin of mine ; *she* used to pull me up when I got on the wrong track. Heigh ho ! I sometimes wonder if the dear old father hadn't interfered—whether Louisa and I . . . No, hang it !—a girl who could lend herself to such a bargain, even send me a sort of message—as I gathered—about her money and the title I may some day inherit, in fact throw herself at a fellow's head—Eugh, she'd be dear at any price. She was such a trump though in those days—seemed so good, and true-hearted ; I hate to think of her, turned, I dare say, into a worldly-wise—fast—forward . . . It's horrid—I'll forget her ; indeed, I had forgotten her, until, somehow, this girl ! Now for it [*putting his leg over the wall*]. Exit the Wolf, minus the Lamb . . . What's that noise ? [*looking round*] somebody walking on tip-toe—Why, as I'm alive, it's my lit . . . my tall friend again. I mustn't throw away an opportunity of advancing in the paths of virtue, under her guidance . . . What on earth is she doing ? I'd better make myself scarce for the moment [*disappears over the wall*].

[LOUISA *returns, smoothing the gravel with her foot as she comes, to hide the mark of footsteps* . . . GEORGE *on the other side of the wall peeps over.*]

GEORGE. Ah ! I understand . . . she's got her wits about her, for all she looks so demure.

LOUISA. How lucky I thought of it in time . . . Miss Wilcox would have ferreted it out . . . a man's footsteps. [*Aside*] They've all gone in to supper, and I've excused myself on the plea of headache, so I'm safe ; and oh, what fun I mean to have ! . . . Won't I get a rise out of Master George when next I see him . . . that's all ! I felt as if I knew him . . . a few years and huge moustaches have certainly altered him, but there's the old smile. I'm furious with him of course. But I used always to end by forgiving him. He was such a dear! and devoted to me!—though he pretended to look down upon me—after the manner of boys; but, the idea of saying he would rather be hanged than marry me! The cheek of it! As if I had the smallest intention of marrying him. Oh! I'll pay him off yet.

GEORGE [*putting his leg over the wall, whistles; she starts*].

LOUISA. What's that?

GEORGE [*whistles again*].

LOUISA. Oh! it's you, is it?

GEORGE. Yes, it's me. May I say a word?

LOUISA. No, you mayn't. Go away!

GEORGE. I am going. But before we part [*sentimentally*], I entreat you to tell me to whom I am indebted for the happy time . . . ?

LOUISA [*suppressing her laughter*]. Happy time, Captain Lister?

GEORGE. No, no; of course it's been a miserable time; but you softened the blow by your kindness. [*Suddenly recollecting, with surprise*] How did you know I was Captain, though?

LOUISA. Why, didn't you send a message to Mary, that Captain Lister—

GEORGE [*interrupting*]. No, no; I said George Lister. Why, I only got my promotion a week ago.

LOUISA [*aside*]. And my uncle wrote to tell me of it at once, for he goes on hankering after his precious plan for us . . . What a goose I am; I'm safe to show myself up. [*Aloud*] Your moustachios speak for themselves!

GEORGE. For themselves, but not for their captain . . . However, surely now you know so much about *me*, you can't refuse to let me know more about *you*?

LOUISA. At any rate, I've not got *my* promotion.

GEORGE [*offended*]. Oh, you are laughing at me! I'd better be off. [*He begins to get over the wall, when a dog barks violently, and he jumps back again.*]

LOUISA. Well?

GEORGE [*astride on the wall*]. Well, Miss Thompson—Johnson. [*Aside*] It's so idiotic not to know the name of a girl who'd heard of one's promotion as soon as one did oneself . . . [*Aloud*] Smithson—

Jackson! [*Aside*] She'll get in a rage in a minute, and let it out. [*Aloud*] The dog's evidently savage, and I've no fancy for being bitten.

LOUISA [*coolly*]. None of those names belong to me, and if you speak gently to the dog, perhaps he won't eat you up; at any rate you must go, for somebody might come by at any minute, and I should get—

GEORGE. Punished?

LOUISA. Severely. And I shall owe my punishment to you. Do go, please.

GEORGE [*aside*]. Bother the girl. She looks so pretty. But it's as clear as a pikestaff that she's laughing at me. [*Keeps looking at her*] Oh, she's distractingly pretty. [*Aloud*] One moment, and I'm gone. [*Sentimentally*] Did it ever happen to you to meet a perfect stranger, and at the end of half an hour to feel as if you had known that person for years . . . and to hope that . . .

LOUISA [*shaking her head slowly and demurely*]. Never.

GEORGE. I feel that sensation now with you . . . I feel as if we were old friends, and I've so many things to say to you . . .

Louisa. For Mary Trevor, of course ?

George [*irritated*]. No, not for Mary Trevor . . . [*After a minute he bursts out laughing.*]

Louisa. What in the world are you laughing at ?

George. When I think of this adventure I can't help it; it's just like me . . . to come here full of one idea . . . and of one person and then not to be able to tear myself away, because I'm full of another idea . . . and of . . . another person.

Louisa [*piqued*]. To increase your amusement I'll go away and send some one else to you . . . *that'll* give you another idea . . . about a third person . . . and so on through the whole school, if there's time . . .

George. Oh no ; I swear to you that this time . . . I am serious.

Louisa. You were never serious in your life, and never will be . . .

George. I ! . . How can you know anything about me, as you never saw me before ?

Louisa [*aside*]. Nearly caught ! [*Aloud*] But I've heard plenty about you. You seem to forget that you've a cousin here . . .

George. Good heavens ! so I have—I'd quite forgotten her . . .

Louisa. Well ! she has not forgotten you . . . for she has often told me . . . .

George [*interrupting*]. Does she know I refused to marry her ?

Louisa. Oh, yes, and she's intensely amused at the notion, and at your thinking you could ever have had the chance.

George [*piqued*]. I fail to see in what way that notion was so intensely amusing. But what else has she told you about me ?

LOUISA. Before I tell you anything, I want to know what makes you dislike her ?

GEORGE. I never said I disliked her.

LOUISA. A man doesn't generally refuse a girl he likes.

GEORGE. A man generally doesn't have the chance of refusing a girl—but there . . . for goodness' sake don't let's talk about her.

LOUISA. Just tell me how it all was, or else I won't tell you what she said.

GEORGE [*impatiently*]. We'd been children together, and, and, when I came back from college, she had gone to school . . .

LOUISA. Well ?

GEORGE. Then my father suggested that I should marry her. Such an idea ! " Thanks," said I. " I'd rather—"

LOUISA. Be hanged . . ?

GEORGE. You appear to know a great deal about it ?

LOUISA. Of course, Louisa told me everything, but just now you seemed to think the idea was not so absurd . . . You wondered why she found it amusing.

GEORGE. Just so ; I can't see what she found amusing . . .

LOUISA. Oh, yes, I see—only amusing . . . for you. But what was she like ? She is—ra-ther pretty now. [*Looks down bashfully.*]

GEORGE. I daresay—in a milk-and-watery sort of way.

LOUISA. And clever too—most people think—

GEORGE. Flippant probably. . . But don't let's go on talking of anything so uninteresting. Just tell me what she said of me, and then . . .

LOUISA [*provokingly*]. Then you have some curiosity about her ?

GEORGE. Not the smallest. It isn't a question of her—but of you —I want to know what impression *you* received—though I can't suppose you'd be influenced by the opinion of one so inferior—so . . .

LOUISA [*aside*]. You're overacting your part, my friend. You're not as indifferent as you think, or as you wish to make me think. . . . [*Aloud*] It's odd you should speak in that bitter tone of one who is so uninteresting. Have you never seen her since ?

GEORGE. Never ! I've taken good care of that. . . I might have been snapped up against my will . . .

LOUISA. Should you know her again, if you came across her ?

GEORGE. Know her ? Of course I should.

LOUISA. Girls of that age do change. Perhaps she has turned out better-looking than you expected.

GEORGE. As you say, girls do change, particularly when they put birdsnests on their foreheads. . . I'm sure you don't do anything so absurd. But with that big hat you hardly let one see you. . . Pray take it off. [*Looks at her tenderly.*] . . . Then you won't tell me ?

LOUISA [*briskly*]. Oh, yes, I will. . . Well, she told me—first— that you've neither heart nor—head.

GEORGE [*huffy*]. Oh, that's first—and what's second ?

LOUISA. Secondly, that you're flighty ; just like a weathercock— I forget the rest, but there was something else. Oh, yes, I remember, Louisa said, If you ever come across him . . . avoid him like poison ; for . . . he don't care what he says of girls . . . boasts about them. I think, Captain Lister, I agree with Louisa there. . .

GEORGE. No, no, no. Don't say that. It's the last thing— there's a reason in her case. Oh ! why did you insist on talking about her ?

LOUISA. Well, never mind now. But do you want to hear any-thing more ?

GEORGE. Yes ; I want to hear what opinion you've formed of me yourself. Tell me candidly of my faults . . . I would alter anything— do anything to please you.

LOUISA [*maliciously*].   Hadn't you better see your cousin first and ask her about me ?

GEORGE.   No ; after what you've told me I wish neither to see her nor to hear of her ; because I didn't want to marry her—is that a reason that she should paint me to you in the blackest colours ?

LOUISA [*laughing*].   I don't think she has any reason to paint you in bright ones ; but before I give you my own opinion—as you wish—pray remember that I've known your cousin from, from . . . her birth . . .

GEORGE.   And loved her no doubt.   That's just like girls.   I dare-say you think her perfection ?

LOUISA.   No ; because then she'd be detestable, and as it is, she's charming ; at any rate, I know her thoroughly—which is more than you seem to do—in spite of having been intimate with her in old days.   And what's more, I know what she felt about you, and how she would have behaved if you had not treated her as you have done.

GEORGE [*trying to appear indifferent*].   Well, let's hear it all, and after that—perhaps you'll leave off harping upon this tiresome cousin.

LOUISA [*beginning by laughing and gradually softening*].   Listen, then. . . . Your cousin agreed with you that such a marriage would have been most undesirable . . . in fact she hated the idea quite as much as you did.

GEORGE [*aside, piqued*].   The devil she did !

LOUIS.   Eh ?

GEORGE.   Nothing, pray go on.

LOUISA.   She would have joined with you in entreating your father to give up the idea.   Still she *had* loved you dearly, and in exchange for that childish love she would have given you the sincerest friendship . . . the warmest affection . . . an affection that would have defied the lapse of years and would have stood by you through life . . . [*All this time George shows signs of emotion.*] Go back in memory to your childhood. Your cousin was younger than you; but didn't she learn the same lessons in order to help you? Didn't she stand between you and your punishments . . . often taking the blame on herself to spare you? During the long illness you had . . . didn't she give up all her little pleasures to sit by your bedside, to read to you, to sing your favourite songs? How she loved you in those far-off times . . . and how have you rewarded her? [*Louisa, too, has been much moved by the revival of old memories, but now gets indignant.*]

How dared you suppose that she was ready to marry you against your will, as you chivalrously remarked just now? How dared you presume that her love for you had changed from that pure sisterly affection! worse still—that she would have given herself to you—unasked—at your father's wish, and valued herself as a thing to be sold to the highest bidder? [*By this time Louisa has worked herself into a flaming passion.*]

GEORGE [*leaning his head on his hands and showing great*

D

emotion]. Didn't I tell you that your influence would make of me whatever you pleased ? You've already crushed out my self-conceit. I could fancy it was Louisa herself speaking : she used to lecture me, and often made me ashamed of myself, as I am now. It's too true ! I've been selfish, conceited, all that she painted me. Ah ! how well I remember those dear old days, and if I had seen her again, and known her as she promised to become . . . the truest-hearted, noblest creature that ever was created ; how different my life might have been ! Perhaps she too would have let the old affection ripen into something warmer, and in making my father happy—we might . . . have been happy ourselves.

LOUISA. Why, then, did you not let those memories speak for her ? Why did you humiliate her and yourself too, for surely those suspicions were unworthy of you both ?

GEORGE. Indeed they were. But my dear old father has something to answer for in that . . . a man naturally hates having any woman offered to him. I ought to have known Louisa better, but my father, in his anxiety for our marriage, expatiated on its worldly advantages, and gave me to understand that she . . . in short he contrived to turn my old affection for Louisa into aversion—if not contempt . . . I was angry—with her—with myself—and perhaps the lowering of the ideal I had formed of her and of what she would become . . . was the real cause of the soreness you noticed . . . Well, it's too late now, and my life is spoilt every way—for I can never hope that you . . .

LOUISA [*hesitating and shy*]. Why is it too late ? Perhaps if your cousin knew that you still . . . I mean that you saw the injustice of your suspicions, and repented of them . . . she might . . . yet . . .

GEORGE [*interrupting her*]. I deserve that you should think me the weather-cock your words imply . . . ready to go through the whole school, as you said. No ! I was speaking of what might have

been before to-day. And yet let me say one word in my own
defence. . . It was just after I received that impression about Louisa,
that I met Mary Trevor . . . it was a mere flirtation between us—
each having gone through a disagreeable episode we were trying to
forget—and if I hadn't accidentally heard that she was being forced
into a marriage she hated—we should probably never have thought of
each other again . .. Then I came to . . . know you [*Louisa laughs*] ;
oh! yes, you are laughing because I've only known you for less than
an hour . . . Well, what of that? However, I won't attempt to argue
the matter. But it's the truth . . . from the first moment, I seemed
to have known you for years . . . laugh as you will, I swear to you
. . . that you reminded me of my cousin in the days when I loved her
so well . . . when her gentle influence could bring out the little good
there was in me. There! I'm only making myself ridiculous and
. . . besides—you think me utterly heartless. Yet when we parted—
Louisa and I—we exchanged rings . . . and in all the years that have
gone by . . . I never took mine off night or day until . . .

LOUISA. Until ?

GEORGE. Until I thought I had cause . . . to—well, to despise
her.

LOUISA. She never took hers off . . . even when she . . .
knew she had cause to . . . despise . . . you.

GEORGE. Ah! I lost a treasure—I know it now.

LOUISA. Then why not . . . try to regain . . . the treasure ?

GEORGE. Because my heart is now irrevocably fixed . . . [*takes
her hand*]; although I fear there is no hope for me.

LOUISA [*leaving her hand in his and pointing to the ring*]. Take
care, you hurt me, you're pressing that ring into my finger.

GEORGE. Poor little finger ! [*examines it, and sees the ring, and
starts back*]. How in the world did you get that ring ?

LOUISA. This ring ? Oh! it was Lousia's, and . . . she—she—
gave it me.

GEORGE [*suspicion dawning on him and his face lighting up*]. Why, you said just now that she never took it off her finger.

LOUISA [*hastily*]. No more she did—I mean—well, if you must know [*defiantly*], I am Louisa.

GEORGE. You—oh, I see it all now—what an ass I've been!— Louisa, darling, remember how we used to love each other—*can* you forgive me?

LOUISA. Well, George, I suppose I must try.

CURTAIN.

HOW HAPPY COULD I BE
WITH EITHER!

~~~~~~~~

Characters.

Mr. Tremayne.
Lady Susan Dering   .   .   *A young Widow.*
Agnes Trevor   .   .   .   *Her Niece.*

Scene :—*A drawing-room at a country house—a door at the back—a door on either side, each having a portière—a chair on the left, on which is a half-finished piece of embroidery—a sofa on the right, near a table, on which are materials for water-colour drawing, and a half-finished sketch.*

[*Enter* Agnes *and* Lady Susan *at different doors.*]

Lady S.   Well! has the post brought any news ?

Agnes.   Absolutely none.   Only two visiting cards—one for you, Aunt Susan, the other for me.

Lady S.   "Mr. Tremayne."   What!   Not contented with his daily visits, he must needs follow them up with bits of pasteboard. Our neighbour is becoming a nuisance.

Agnes.   There I agree ; but why do you encourage him ?

Lady S.   I encourage him ?   That's good!   It's rather you, my dear, who do that.

Agnes.   Not I.   But I've got eyes in my head.

Lady S.   And I've got ears in mine.   But granted that I may have been civil to Mr. Tremayne. What then? You have certainly not been backward in welcoming his visits.

AGNES. I?

LADY S. [*continuing*]. Besides, it's no secret to you, that I'm already half-engaged. . . . Poor Victor! how constant he has been!

AGNES. Pshaw! My dear aunt, I beg to say that I never believed in your attachment to Victor. Why, didn't I hear you tell him that the widow of a consul-general couldn't possibly marry any one below the rank of a captain? It's now two years since he sailed for Africa. My belief is that you've completely forgotten poor Victor, and that it would be folly in him to cherish any hope of becoming—

LADY S. A captain!

AGNES. No! the husband of a woman capable of giving such an answer . . . an answer that you certainly would not have given to Mr. Tremayne.

LADY S. You think so?

AGNES. I am sure of it. I couldn't help seeing your delight this morning, at getting a letter [*pointedly*] brought—by—hand!

LADY S. Which you believe to have been from Mr. Tremayne, followed by his cards? I should like to know what possible reason he could have for doing so stupid a thing.

AGNES. How should I know? But it wouldn't be the first time that excessive caution has overreached itself.

LADY S. That presumption, my dear, is—to say the least of it—rash; for [*sarcastically*] though Mr. Tremayne overwhelms *us* with visits—inundates *us* with attentions—nothing, absolutely nothing, in his manner indicates a preference for one over the other.

AGNES. That I admit. . . . Indeed, he takes pains not to pronounce—outwardly, at any rate—in favour of either.

LADY S. It remains, then, to be seen which of us is the most susceptible to *his* fascinations.

AGNES. I, for one, haven't the smallest doubt on that point.

Lady S.   Strange perversity.   However, to prove to you that I care no more for our neighbour than you pretend to do, if he should call to-day—

Agnes.   After sending his cards ?

Lady S.   They were probably the forerunners.   The weather prevents our stirring out, and Mr. Tremayne makes considerable use of his opportunities—in saving us from the horrors of solitude.

Agnes.   Well, we'll take for granted that he calls.   What next ?

LADY S. What next ? Why, after an arctic reception, we'll make some transparent excuse to get rid of him. I suppose he'll take the hint, and spare us somewhat of his society in future.

AGNES. Surely this would be very uncivil.

LADY S. Oh ! if *you* have any scruples or qualms.

AGNES. I ! none whatever. But how about yourself ? Are you certain that you may not repent and regret later on ?

LADY S. Aha ! Take care, or I may think you are speaking of *yourself.*

AGNES. Then you'll think wrong. Meantime, *I* shall leave the room at once, hoping [*with emphasis*] that the poor man may find it empty if he does come. [*Aside*] At least that'll be better than being ignominiously turned out.   [*Exit.*]

LADY S. So, so, my little niece ! If you go on snubbing every possible husband, you'll end in being an old maid. Happily for you, it was not lightly that I undertook to replace, as far as I could, a mother's care, though I can only pretend to the influence of a sister, as our ages are so nearly the same. This Mr. Tremayne seems to be everything I could wish for you, and it's a chance not to be neglected. In these days, eligible husbands are not to be had for the asking, and one little fact encourages my hopes, which is, that the green-eyed monster seems to be already at work ; but whether this may be from love or vanity, I'm not so sure. How shall I set about solving the interesting problem ? [*Walks about meditating.*] Ah ! I have it. By feigning a secret predilection for the Adonis in question ; this will give him the flavour of forbidden fruit—an undoubted point in his favour. I'll keep up this farce in Agnes's presence, and, who knows ?—perhaps sometimes in her absence ! At any rate, that will prevent me from forgetting my part !   [*Exit to right.*]

MR. TREMAYNE [*speaking to some one outside*]. All right, I know my way. [*He enters by the centre door, carrying a book and a roll of music. He goes straight to the place where he supposes* LADY SUSAN *to* be, *and holds out the book.*] Lady Susan, I have brought you [*surprised at not seeing her*]. Ah! [*turning to the left with the roll of music*] Miss Trevor, I . . . No one here? Well, so much the better [*goes to the mantlepiece and puts down the book and the music*]. It gives me time to pull myself together. I'm in a fix! All my ideas get con-fused, and yet nothing can be more genuine than the source of this very confusion—I'm nearly thirty, and after that, a bachelor's fate means not merely independence but isolation. I made a vow to be married before the winter, and I mean it; for I shudder at being reduced to lavish my affections on a dog or a cat, or possibly a canary bird—So I'm on the look-out for a wife who shall unite in her charming person the qualities of all three—no, not the cat! Rather treacherous ladies those! Well, as I was saying, I get muddled and vacillate between this chair and that sofa [*designating the chair on the left and the sofa on the right*]. Miss Agnes fascinates, Lady Susan charms me; I pine for the niece, I sigh for the aunt. On this chair bewitching innocence, on that sofa irre-.sistible wit. There, I'm losing my head again. . . . What is to put an end to it all? If these two lovely creatures weigh equally in the scale of perfection, what can a fellow do but sing, like Macheath, "How happy could I be with either, were t'other dear charmer away"? [*After long cogitation.*] Let chance decide. That's it! I breathe once more! The first who enters this room shall be my choice. To her I will dedicate my life. Oh, the blessed repose of decision after doubt. [*At this moment he sees the portières open at each side.*]

[*Enter* Agnes *and* Lady Susan *simultaneously*].

Gracious powers, what will become of me? [*Turning and appealing to the audience*] I can't marry them both, can I?

Mr. Tremayne [*making two low bows*]. Lady Susan . . . Miss Trevor. [*They seat themselves after making formal curtseys.*] [*Aside*] Ceremony seems the order of the day. [*After an awkward pause*] I fear I was not expected. [*Embarrassed.*] Indeed, I myself had not intended—Let me at least ask you how you are ?

LADY S. [*on the right*]. How we are ?

MR. TREMAYNE. I—was—asking—

LADY S. and AGNES [*both together*]. We are both quite well, thanks for your kind inquiries. [*They sit down facing the audience, one occupied with her embroidery, the other with her drawing.*]

MR. TREMAYNE [*aside*]. A charming picture ! But the situation decidedly strained. [*Aloud*] I—I went into Plymouth this morning, hoping to render a slight service to—each of you . . . [*He takes the book and music from the mantlepiece. Turning to* LADY SUSAN] Here is the novel you were asking about ; [*to* AGNES] and here the new song you were wishing for. [*Takes other things out of his pocket*]. [*To* LADY SUSAN] Some scent from Benson's ; [*to* AGNES] chocolates from Loveland's ; [*to* LADY SUSAN] the *Times* for you, [*to* AGNES] and for you the *Queen*.

LADY S. [*aside*]. Not a hint as to which he prefers.

AGNES [*aside*]. Impossible to guess—this is unbearable.

MR. TREMAYNE [*puzzled by the silence, aside.*] What does it all mean ? [*He gets up, walks about, then seizes a stool and places it between them and sits resolutely down.*] [*Aloud*] This is a very pleasant reception for the most devoted admirer of—of both of you [*gets up excitedly*]. I must be blind not to perceive it. Total silence is not [*sarcastically*] your usual way. I am evidently in disgrace ; but may I ask how I have offended ?

LADY S. [*with a coquettish air*]. Oh ! offended.

AGNES [*the same*]. Offended ; oh !

LADY S. [*resuming the ironical tone*]. You who are so amiable to us *both*.

AGNES [*the same.*] So kind to us *both*.

LADY S. A slave to *our* caprices.

AGNES. A victim to *our* whims.

LADY S.   Pray believe, on the contrary, in *our* friendship.

AGNES.   In *our* gratitude.

[*During this dialogue they speak very rapidly, almost together.*]

MR. TREMAYNE.   You really overwhelm me, but you must know that I have but one object in life, which is—to be permitted . . . order

me, command me.   Is there nothing I can do to amuse you ?   Shall we try a little music ?

LADY S.   I hate music.

AGNES.   So do I.

MR. TREMAYNE.   Shall I read aloud ?

LADY S. and AGNES [*both together*].   Oh yes, do.

MR. TREMAYNE.   What shall I read ?

LADY S.   Aha! We've caught him now.
AGNES.   We'll make this the test.

[*Each gives him a paper and speak together.*]

AGNES and LADY S. [*together*]. }   The *Queen*.
                                     The *Times*.

MR. TREMAYNE [*a paper in each hand, aside*].   Hang it all, I shall

be driven to do something desperate ; but I won't allow myself to be caught—not I.

LADY S. and AGNES [*together*]. Well!

MR. TREMAYNE. Now for the *Times*.

LADY S. and AGNES [*together*]. Ah !

MR. TREMAYNE. And now for the *Queen*.

LADY S. and AGNES [*together*]. Ah !

MR. TREMAYNE [*aside*]. Landed! [*Aloud, reads out sentences alternately and very quickly from each paper.*]

"As regards the suppression of the slave trade, no object can be more desirable"—"The best recipe for orange marmalade is as follows"—"and to civilize Central Africa would be"—"Take the rind off seven Maltese oran—"   .

AGNES and LADY S. [*both together, and stopping their ears*]. There, for mercy's sake, stop!

MR. TREMAYNE. Enchanted to obey. [*Folds up the papers. A long silence follows. Much embarrassed, he looks from one to the*

other, then gets up, pushes away the stool, and approaches AGNES.]
What marvellous embroidery! [*turning to* LADY SUSAN] what exquisite
painting! The one embroiders with her brush, the other paints with
her needle.

LADY S. [*in a soft, coquettish voice*]. You are really too
flattering.

MR. TREMAYNE [*with a tender ac-
cent*]. Have I not to make my peace?

AGNES [*furious*]. So like my aunt
—trying to monopolize him.

LADY S. You know too well that
I cannot be angry with *you*—for long.

MR. TREMAYNE [*completely for the
moment forgetting his double part,
aside*]. Ah! what eyes! what grace!
[*Aloud, energetically*] Ah! Lady
Susan.

AGNES [*aside, deeply agitated*]. Oh!

MR. TREMAYNE [*a-
side, with conviction*].
Here is my choice—the
idol whom I adore [*kisses
the hand* LADY SUSAN
holds out].

AGNES [*exasperated, aside*]. Then this is to be the end of it. My
aunt has positively fastened herself upon him. It's disgusting, and at
her age, too! But I'll have my turn. [*Aloud, with a faint scream*]
Ah!

MR. TREMAYNE [*rushing to her side*]. What is it?

AGNES. The needle pricked me. Oh! Oh!

LADY S. The needle, or . . . something else?

Mr. Tremayne [*seizing* Agnes's *hand*]. I can't bear to see you suffer.

Agnes [*in a doleful tone*]. It does hurt so. Oh! take care.

Mr. Tremayne [*examining her hand*]. There's nothing to be seen . . . except, indeed [*tenderly*] a lovely little hand.

Lady S. [*aside*]. I hope the wound is deeper than that.

Agnes [*coquettishly*]. How kind you are, to care about my poor hand.

Mr. Tremayne [*again forgetting his double part*]. Kind! Happy, you mean, to be able . . . too happy.

Lady S. [*aside*]. I begin to think the man must be a fool. Or does he care for her?

Agnes [*aside*]. My aunt's furious. [*Aloud*] How can I thank you enough?

Mr. Tremayne [*aside*]. Those tender accents thrill me, and what eyes! I'm now convinced that my heart is given irrevocably to Agnes. [*He half turns and sees* Lady Susan, *who has placed herself before him. Aside.*] Oh! bother. [*He retires up the stage.*] I'm falling between two stools.

Lady S. [*turning on* Agnes, *and speaking in a low voice*]. Is this the way you adhere to our compact?

Agnes [*the same*]. I like that when you—

Lady S. [*interrupting her*]. You can't deny that you flirt with him?

Agnes. Not more than you do, anyhow.

Mr. Tremayne [*aside*]. What on earth can they be whispering about?

Lady S. [*continuing to whisper*]. Well, I shall now leave the room, and I think you had better—

Agnes [*interrupting her. The same*]. Don't be the least afraid, I shall follow you.

Mr. Tremayne [*aside, watching them both*]. I'll be hanged if I know which I do prefer. . . The last I speak to carries the day. . . The only thing to be done now is to try and ascertain if either of them wishes to marry me ! as I, clearly, wish to marry them both.

LADY S. [*whispering to* AGNES]. Then it's decided, and I begin . . . [*putting her hands to her head and groaning. Aloud*]. Oh ! my head !

MR. TREMAYNE [*eagerly running to her*]. What's the matter ?

LADY S. Sudden neuralgia—it's torture.

MR. TREMAYNE [*sympathetically*]. Is there nothing I can do ? I can't bear to see you suffer. Won't it soon pass off ?

LADY S. Ah ! no [*speaking as if in great pain*] when once these attacks come on, I am laid up for a week. So sorry to be obliged to leave you.   [*Exit on right.*]

MR. TREMAYNE [*aside, disconcerted*]. It's a very remarkable neuralgia—so sudden too.

AGNES [*aside*]. My turn now, but what excuse can I find to leave him ?

MR. TREMAYNE [*aside*]. The aunt escapes me—but the niece remains. [*Aloud*] Miss Trevor. . . .

AGNES [*hesitating*]. My poor little birds . . . they've had nothing to eat for two days . . .

MR. TREMAYNE. Then they must be dead long ago . . .

AGNES. Oh, Mr. Tremayne, how can you say such a horrible thing [*backing to the door*]. I should never forgive myself. . . . I mustn't lose a moment. Excuse my leaving you so abruptly. Good-bye. [*She goes out on the left side.*]

MR. TREMAYNE. Confound it . . . neuralgia, birds—birds, neuralgia—what does it all mean ? I arrive—they basket me for no earthly reason—then suddenly vie with each other in amiability, and then—disappear altogether ! Do they expect me to disappear too, I wonder ? Not I—I'm exasperated, and nothing shall make me leave this house until I'm engaged to one of them—unless, indeed, both should

LADY S.   I'll walk with you as far as the gate.

MR. TREMAYNE [*in consternation*]. Pray do not. Don't think of it.

LADY S. [*aside*]. Ah! I begin to see daylight . . . I trust I'm not mistaken.

MR. TREMAYNE [*bowing*]. Then I take my leave. [*Aside*] She is more beautiful than ever! How well this quiet dignity suits her. [*Exit.*]

LADY S. [*alone*]. I must keep a good look out, for there's something I can't, for the life of me, understand. [*Exit at the right-hand door.*]

MR. TREMAYNE [*who has watched the departure of Lady Susan, returns on tip-toe, rubbing his hands joyfully*]. . . . The plot's thickening—here comes Miss Trevor, and then for the catastrophe . . .

AGNES [*coming in quietly from the left*]. Surely I heard voices?

MR. TREMAYNE [*turning his back quickly and making the same by-play as with Lady Susan before, and kissing his hand towards* LADY SUSAN'S *room*]. Adorable creature!

AGNES.   What do I see? [*Disgusted.*]

MR. TREMAYNE [*pretending astonishment and embarrassment*]. Oh! heavens, it is Miss Trevor [*falling on his knees before her*].

AGNES [*with dignity*]. Mr. Tremayne.

MR. TREMAYNE. Oh, say that you do not love me.

AGNES [*recoiling*] Eh? . . .

MR. TREMAYNE. Oh, I repeat it, tell me that I am indifferent to you or I shall never dare to—

AGNES [*interrupting him, and recoiling still further from him coldly*]. Pray explain yourself . . .

MR. TREMAYNE. How can I explain? Oh! the torture of feeling that I may have caused you unhappiness. Forgive me—I did not understand myself till too late.

AGNES. This is extraordinary language.

MR. TREMAYNE. Then you do not care for me? Thank heaven! then I may without remorse find my happiness with another. But let me hear it from your own lips—Assure me that you do not care for me!

AGNES [*aside and deeply moved*]. This is too dreadful.

MR. TREMAYNE. Oh! Agnes, forgive me, and leave me, I implore you.

AGNES [*in a state of stupefaction*]. I—I—you ask me to—

MR. TREMAYNE. Yes, as a last favour—do not stay here . . .

AGNES [*aside*]. Is he expecting my aunt? What terrible humiliation . . .

MR. TREMAYNE [*aside, examining her attentively*]. She's more affected than her aunt appeared to be . . .

AGNES [*angrily*]. I'm only too glad to leave you—[*much agitated, aside*] the wretch, the monster! [*Exit at the door on the left.*]

MR. TREMAYNE. She is furious . . . and how lovely she looks in her rage! [*noise of china falling*] admirable . . . now for the climax . . . [*a pause*] . . . Profound silence, too profound to be natural, with daughters of Eve! curiosity, if not jealousy, will come to the rescue . . . [*Listens attentively, and then in a low voice, pointing to the portières, which show slight movements.*] Didn't I say so? There they are. Oh! little god of love—Cupid! to my aid.

LADY S. [*just visible to the audience, behind the portière, not daring to advance*]. I must hear what they say to each other.

AGNES [*same by-play*]. I mustn't lose a word of what those two are saying.

E 2

Mr. Tremayne [*having ascertained that no one can see what passes, comes forward to the centre. A dialogue ensues between himself in his natural voice and his imitation of the supposed voice of a woman, which must be made very comic*]. Ah! you're trembling—for pity's sake be calm and listen—[*interrupting*] [*Woman's voice*] Oh! if we were discovered, I should die. [*Natural voice.*] Don't be afraid, have confidence in me. [*Woman's voice.*] Oh, Mr. Tremayne! [*Natural voice.*] Ineffable joy! To think that this cruel indifference was but assumed to conceal from others the blessed truth—was it not? Oh!—

 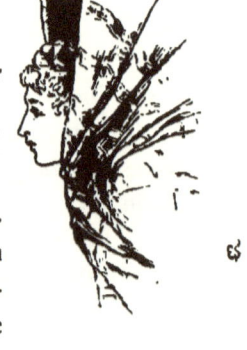

let me hear it from your own lips—[*Woman's voice.*] Ah, yes.

Agnes [*from behind the curtain, indignant*]. Oh!

Lady S. [*the same*]. I couldn't have believed it!

Mr. Tremayne [*continuing in his own voice*]. You love me, then! Angel, a-dored one . . . My whole life is yours . . . at your feet I throw myself. [*He kisses his own hand vehemently.*]

Agnes [*half-opening the curtain*]. Outrageous, horrible, disgusting.

Lady S. [*almost at the same moment*]. . . . This is an insult . . . [*At this moment they both show themselves, but still hold the curtain, ready to retreat at the first alarm—each starts back indignant at the sight of the other, and both speak in exasperated tones.*]

Agnes. And so *you*, my aunt, have been grossly deceiving me?

Lady S. And *you*, who should show respect and confidence to your aunt—you think to make me your dupe by pretending to have just entered the room.   Fie, you should be ashamed of yourself.   [*She advances into the room.*]

AGNES [*also advancing*].   What do you mean ?

LADY S.   Disgraceful ! . . . A girl of your age to make a clan-destine appointment with a young man . . .

AGNES.   You dare to accuse me of making clandestine appoint-ments, when I've just found *you*—in spite of all your protestations of indifference—here with Mr. Tremayne ; oh ! don't take the trouble to deny it, I heard all that passed.

LADY S.   Your insolence passes belief . . . So you are trying to carry the war into the enemy's camp, by pretending that *I* was the heroine in the farce that has just been enacted.

AGNES [*ironically*].   And who else, pray, could have been the enactor of the farce ?

LADY S. [*suppressing with difficulty an explosion of anger*]. Enough of this, if you please.   As to you [*turning to* TREMAYNE], I believed you to be a gentleman, or you would never have been received into my house—As it is, I must beg you for the future—

MR. TREMAYNE [*interrupting, having in vain been trying to inter-pose*].   I must be allowed to speak, or my life will be passed in vain regrets—in misery untold.

AGNES.   You had better not.   Your treachery is sufficiently clear already.

LADY S. [*severely, and in good faith, turning to* AGNES].   Don't be a hypocrite.

MR. TREMAYNE.   I must insist on being heard—

LADY S.   I beg you will say no more—and again I must ask you to leave my house.

AGNES.   Yes, Mr. Tremayne, you had better, as my aunt says, leave the house.   But before we part—never, I trust, to meet again— you shall learn the truth.   You spoke of regrets—of misery—what cause *you* have for such feelings, I know not—But [*a pause*] as this is

the last time we shall meet, I am not ashamed to confess my weakness. You did your utmost to gain my affections . . . and [*turning away*] you—you—succeeded [*puts her handkerchief to her eyes and walks away*].

MR. TREMAYNE [*ecstatically*]. Can it be possible? Do I understand that you could have loved me?

AGNES [*gravely, turning towards him*]. Yes, Mr. Tremayne. I could have placed my happiness in your hands—I could have—[*getting excited*]—Oh! heavens, what folly—but it's all over, and now—far from loving—I hate you, Mr. Tremayne, I hate you.

LADY S. [*aside*]. I can't make it out. [*Aloud*] This is an interesting avowal, no doubt, but scarcely necessary, I should think, after the little episode I witnessed just now?

AGNES [*infuriated*]. This hypocrisy is revolting. You know that it was I who found you both out, and I can never, never forgive you.

LADY S. [*thoroughly puzzled and annoyed, to* AGNES]. You force me by your obstinacy to a disagreeable step. [*To* MR. TREMAYNE] I must call upon you to declare the truth—

MR. TREMAYNE. My dear Lady Susan, I have been trying in vain to declare it all this time—I love Miss Trevor with my whole heart. The happiness of my life depends upon her becoming my wife. May I dare to hope that I am not altogether indifferent to her? [*turning to* AGNES].

LADY S. [*joyfully*]. At last my dearest wish is accomplished.

AGNES [*turning to* LADY SUSAN, *angrily*]. You!—my rival?

LADY S. A pretended rival, dear child! [*a pause*] so you really believe I had forgotten my poor Victor! [*showing her a letter*] Captain Victor will be here to-morrow.

AGNES [*scarcely convinced*]. Then what was the meaning of the interview between you and Mr. Tremayne?

LADY S. [*impatiently*]. Don't let's have any more of that folly.

MR. TREMAYNE [*in the centre*]. I must now make my confession

. . . [*imitates again a woman's voice*] Ah! Mr. Tremayne, yes! [*and then kisses his own hand violently*].

LADY S. and AGNES [*both together, laughing*]   But what was it all for?

MR. TREMAYNE.   Ah! don't let us talk of causes—the result is—for myself, at least, the perfection of happiness.

CURTAIN.

WELL MATCHED AFTER ALL.

Characters.

GENERAL SIR HENRY MILMAN.
MARGARET, *his Wife.*
ROONEY, *an old Irish Soldier Servant.*

SCENE:—*A Drawing-room profusely decorated with flowers, portières and hangings, pictures, armchairs, sofas, &c., opening on to a garden, with a large mirror at one side of the room.* MARGARET *discovered, dressed in white muslin and a broad pink sash, and on one of the sofas a little straw hat with a bunch of pink rose-buds.*

MARGARET. [*A basket of flowers in her hand, contemplating the room.*] There, that's something like. One wouldn't know the room again. Can I ever forget my feelings when I first saw it? White and gold paper, carpet with a huge pattern in every colour of the rainbow, great ugly doors, and staring windows. Now, what with pictures, armchairs, portières, the hideous carpet covered with felt, and, above all, flowers; flowers in every niche and corner; it's really quite habitable. Ugh! how tired I am! [*Throws herself on a sofa.*] Is there anything so exhausting as arranging flowers, and upsetting furniture? [*Throws her arms over her head. A pause.*] Yes, there's something much worse; upsetting my blessed old General and his blessed old habits; and that's what I've got to do. I'm getting rather frightened. To think of arranging a garden party this afternoon without even telling him. But, if I had told him, he would have been sure to say "No;" and then!—It's in his interest as much as my own, and he can't be more bored with it than I shall be. [*She pulls a news paper out of her pocket.*] The more I think of this disgusting article the more furious I get. [*She reads out*] "It appears that our new

General, Sir Henry Milman, an old gentleman who does not seem to have carried his sixty years with ease, for he looks even older than he is, has recently married a beautiful girl of eighteen. We trust that the young wife may be able to support her life in this dull place, and that the poor old General may have no cause to repent of his temerity," &c., &c. Brute . . . Though if the man who wrote it saw us getting out of the train I could almost sympathize with his feelings, for the General outdid himself. He really might have been ninety with those horrid old clothes . . . For myself I don't mind a bit. Dear old fellow! I love him far too well, and admire him too much, to care a pin how he dresses. But when he *can* look so well! I hate other people to see him disfigured. How proud I was of him that night at the Duke's. He looked so handsome with his tall, upright figure, and covered with orders. And on our wedding-day, too! But thereby hangs a tale. It's my belief that but for old Rooney and myself he would have appeared in church in the famous suit he's so fond of [*imitates him in a gruff voice*] that "went through three campaigns and five years at the Cape!" It's his mania to make himself look old, and he's very little over fifty in spite of this [*raps the newspaper*]. What's even fifty-five for a man? Why, it's the best possible age! [*Looks at her watch.*] Goodness me, it's nearly two o'clock! He'll be home soon. His family tell me that he can be very savage. I've never seen him angry myself; but I can just fancy he might get into a rage. Sometimes, if I suggest a change in our plans and arrangements, he looks rather cross—and then he has a way of saying, "Oh! pray don't mind me;" or, "Might I venture to ask?"—which sends cold water down my back! Never mind; he's a darling; and he won't throw me over to-day, when he sees I'm bent on his showing himself . . . [*Looks at the paper again.*] Insolent creature! My handsome General to be called an old . . . Oh! I could box the man's ears . . . [*Goes to the door and calls*] Rooney, Rooney!

[*Enter* ROONEY.]*

MARGARET. Have you got all the General's things ready, as I told you? and varnished his boots? and, above all, Rooney, don't forget to cut his hair a little, and do make him wax his moustaches?

ROONEY. Bedad! milady; it'll be waxy all over the Gineral will be when he sees the way he's to be put about; and I'm for thinking he won't like all this nayther [*pointing to the decorations*]; and, saving yer presence, he'll flare up into the divil's own rage!

MARGARET. Nonsense, Rooney. Sir Henry always likes what I like. And as to putting himself into a rage! how dare you say so, Rooney! The General's never angry; or, if he is, other people are sure to be in fault.

ROONEY. Humph! [*with hesitation*]. Bedad and bedad!

MARGARET [*laughing*]. Now, don't go on with your everlasting—Bedad and bedad! [*imitating him*], but listen to me. You love your master, and you're proud of him, or you ought to be—aren't you, Rooney?

ROONEY. It's proud I am of the master—small blame to me—a dale prouder than he is of himself!

* In case there should be a difficulty in acting the part of an Irishman, the character of Rooney has been adapted to that of an English servant, and will be found at the end of the Play.

MARGARET.   And I'm proud of him, and I mean every one to know it, and they shall, too, with your help.   But, dear old Rooney [*coaxingly*], though you and I think there's no one so handsome and grand-looking—still, when people see him for the first time in those

very odd-looking clothes—you know, that old jacket, and those hideous trowsers !

ROONEY.   Shure, milady ! it's them that's gone through the fire and water of three cam—

MARGARET [*interrupting him*].   Oh, yes, I know ; I know ; and I love the old rags. But they're not exactly becoming; and, somehow, he's got a way of stooping when he wears them; and then he let's his hair grow all shaggy. In short [*suddenly exploding*] . . . Now, look at this, Rooney; there's an insolent newspaper [*taking it out of her pocket and pointing to it*], which calls him an old man, and jeers at him for having married a young wife, and dares to insinuate that I . . . Oh! it's too shameful.

ROONEY. The divil take the whole boiling of 'em! I ax yer ladyship's pardon for swearing, but Serjeant Tozer, him that's at the militia quarters, was reading this paper at the canteen, and I up and told him—the ugly varmint, it was trason, and a lie! and that, ould as I am, I'd like to get at the baste as wrote that same. And I'd give him what the boys give the drum at Donnybrook Fair, with a taste of my speech thrown in for nothing!

MARGARET [*laughing*]. That I'm sure you would, Rooney, whatever that dreadful thing may be; but I've thought of a better plan still —to turn the laugh against them all, and to set every one talking of the handsome Sir Henry Milman, and of what an enviable woman his wife must be. Won't that be splendid? [*rubbing her hands with delight*]. So now you'll help me, won't you, Rooney? You know the General lets you do what you like. Why, I've heard him say you're the best barber in England; and that means that you're as good a barber as you're a faithful servant . . . Dear old Rooney!

ROONEY. A close shaver in fact he'll be maning. There now, milady, it's your pretty young self that's coming over an ould fellow wid the blarney of yer beautiful tongue, and there's no going agin you at all—at all!

MARGARET. That's right, Rooney; of course you won't go against me, because all I'm doing, as you well know, is for your dear master's sake. But I think I hear him riding into the stable-yard. Just help me to get these flower-baskets out of the way, and push some of the chairs back. The General has a way of rushing in in a tremendous hurry, and then he stumbles over everything. [*They arrange the furniture.*] [*Aside*] I'm in an awful fright, but I don't mean to let him see it, not I. [*Aloud*] Now run away, Rooney, and get all his things ready.   [*Exit* ROONEY.]

[MARGARET *sits down, with her back to the door, and takes up her work and pretends to be counting the stitches.*]

[*Enter* SIR HENRY.]

SIR HENRY [*dressed in an old jacket, loose trousers, and wearing a large felt hat and a loose tie, with his hair and moustaches untrimmed, comes in very hastily—but stops suddenly, looking round surprised— then goes from one table to another to put down his hat and whip, but finds them all covered with flowers*]. [*Aside*] What the devil does all this mean? [*Throws his hat, &c., on a chair, and then sees* MARGARET] . . . Might I be permitted to inquire the reason for this extraordinary metamorphosis? I thought I lived in a house; but it seems I'm to live in a conservatory!

MARGARET [*turning round*]. Oh! six, seven, eight, nine, there you are! I didn't hear you come in. Had a nice ride, dear? [*She tries to speak indifferently.*]

SIR H. Never mind my ride, but be so kind as to answer my question. . . .

MARGARET [*nervous, but pretending to be quite innocent*] . . . Your question? . . .

SIR H. Yes; I requested to know the reason for this exhibition? Can it be your birthday? If so, that's another thing—but [*looking at her affectionately*] in that case, why didn't you say so, darling, that I might have got something for you?

MARGARET [*aside*]. How I hate vexing him. [*Aloud*] Oh! no;

it's not my birthday. Why should you think so ? [*appearing indifferent*].

SIR H. [*severely*]. Don't be ridiculous, Margaret. You're evading my question. Are you determined not to answer me ?

MARGARET [*innocently surprised*]. Oh! dear no; why shouldn't I answer you? It's . . . my—day !

SIR H. Your day . . . what the deuce do you mean by your day—and why ?

MARGARET [*half crying*]. Look here, Henry, if you're going to swear at me—you never did before—and to ask me the reason for every little thing ; and especially to-day, when I'd such lots of things to . . . I mean when I want you to do such lots of things to please me . . . I couldn't have believed you would be so unkind . . . [*She wipes her eyes*].

SIR H. [*softening*]. Now do be sensible, dearest ! I only ask you the reason for all this? [*pointing to the room and then to her dress*].

MARGARET [*offended*]. Oh! if you don't like this dress; I must say, *I* thought I looked rather nice in it—and hoped that you would think so too [*pouting*].

SIR H. [*looking at her tenderly*]. You look more than nice, little Margaret ! . . . Lovely ! . . . as you always do.

MARGARET. There now, you're like yourself again. Come and sit down, and we'll talk it all over.

SIR H. Easier said than done [*getting cross again*]. Where am I supposed to sit . . . where's my chair ?

MARGARET [*pushing him on a sofa, and sitting down by him*] . . . Now, let's be comfortable. You see, for your sake, we ought to be civil to the neighbours . . . and so . . . I thought a little kind of garden party was the easiest way. [*Aside*] I can't bear to tell him the real reason.

SIR H. But why didn't you tell me this before? [*He gets up.*]

MARGARET. I only remembered it after you'd gone. out . . . [*Aside*] What an awful story! [*Aloud*] But [*getting up and looking at him*] what have you got on? What odd trousers! and this—is it a jacket? I never saw it before. [*She walks round him.*]

SIR H. [*angry*]. The deuce you didn't!—and pray, what's the matter with 'em? They've gone through three campaigns, and five years at the Cape . . . You must be dreaming . . . And what do you mean by walking round me like a captain inspecting his company?

MARGARET [*laughing*]. The captain's not at all satisfied, I can tell you. [*Makes a comical face, at which the General can't help laughing*].

SIR H. Well, do you want to put me under arrest?

MARGARET. No, I'll let you off with a good. scolding this time. But first of all you shall have a little compliment.

SIR H. That's just like a woman . . . First she strokes; then scratches you.

MARGARET [*with a coquettish manner*]. Do you remember the day of our marriage?

SIR H. Yes, it was the 7th of —

MARGARET [*interrupting*]. I don't mean the date; not likely that I should forget that. I'm afraid of making you vain! but I must tell you how proud I was of you that day! . . . You looked quite beautiful! . . . there! And as I walked down the aisle on your arm—I felt that every girl must be envying me. . .

SIR H. [*much affected and flattered*]. You really felt proud of your old husband? Ah! my little Margaret, you were blinded by your own affectionate heart. But what have you thought of him since?

MARGARET. Well! since ?—I think him as handsome as ever, only he doesn't do himself justice. Now look at this room; it's the same that we sat in yesterday; but see the difference, a little care, a few flowers!

SIR H. Perhaps you'd like me to put on a wreath of roses?

MARGARET. No! but I want you to change [*laughing and pointing to his dress*] these memorials of . . . of the Cape!

SIR. H. What! this comfortable jacket and my dear old trousers; what next?

MARGARET. What next? Why, put on a frock coat.

SIR. H. Better say an evening coat at once, while you're about it.

MARGARET. No; a frock coat will do . . . and then you've got to tidy up.

SIR H. And then what am I to do? Dance a fandango? [*mockingly.*]

MARGARET [*very seriously*]. Then you've got to stay with me and help me to receive these people.

SIR H. [*walking about as if to control himself*]. No. Stay with you as much as you like . . . I desire no better. But to dance attendance on all these people, certainly not; I'm not a drawing-room man. . . I'm a soldier [*turning to her*]. Now look you, Margaret, there's something behind all this that I don't understand, I've never known you so unreasonable and so childishly absurd [*working himself up into a passion*].

MARGARET. Unreasonable . . . absurd . . . because I want you to look as—in short, as you did on our wedding day [*by this time she has got agitated and half crying*].

SIR H. [*stops short in his walk and looks at her attentively*] [*aside*]. Ah! now I understand [*after a pause he sits down, takes her hand and strokes it soothingly, while she kneels before him*] [*aloud*]. Poor Margaret, poor child! At the time of our marriage your kind generous nature made

F

you wilfully blind to the terrible discrepancy between us . . . while I, in the selfishness of mine, took advantage of your inexperience [*all this time Margaret tries to interrupt him, but he continues without heeding her*]. Now you have too late awakened to the truth, and you find your youth and beauty tied to a man old enough to be your father—almost your grandfather.

MARGARET [*bounding up, her cheeks in a flame*]. How dare you say such cruel things, and not one word of truth in them ! I'm not a baby, and I haven't married an old man, and I won't be told I have . . . and you can't care for me a bit . . . and . . .

SIR H. [*very gravely interrupting her*]. You have never admitted it yourself, I am certain — and you've been to me all that the fondest heart could desire. But, Margaret, darling, take my advice and don't attempt to lessen the disparity of our years by trying to make anything of me but what I am. Think of me, my little Margaret, as your best, your truest friend . . . as one whose only thought shall be to make you happy, and to shield you as far as possible from trouble ; bear with my old habits and my old clothes, dear [*he laughs*], why, you'd only make me look ridiculous.

MARGARET [*Makes him a curtsey, smiles breaking through her tears, and speaks in her old saucy manner*]. General Sir Henry Milman, commanding the district, you have had your say, and now I mean to have mine . . . I don't admit the truth of one syllable you have been saying, but we won't quarrel about it, we'll make a compact ; to please me you will dress yourself for this afternoon exactly as you did for our wedding, and you will receive the natives for this once ; after that, we shall see who's right and who's wrong, only you must *not* be obstinate or refuse to be convinced. I say that we are a perfectly well assorted couple . . . you pretend that I'm a baby and that you're an antiquated edition of Methuselah, which, by-the-bye, is exceedingly rude to me as well as to the object of my choice, for I beg you to remember that I could have married lots of people, and you ought to respect my taste. There now, go and dress ; I give you just half an hour [*pushes him towards the door*].

SIR H. Very well, you little tyrant, one can bear anything for once, but I've my condition to make also. I must know the reason for this ridiculous pantomime.

MARGARET. You shall know it after you're dressed, if you promise to do all I tell you.

SIR H. Before I go, however, I will just ask you to come with me [*leads her to a long mirror*], I never care to see myself in a looking-glass . . .

MARGARET [*interrupts him vehemently*]. No ; I wish you did—

SIR H. [*he continues*]. But for this once ! Now stand by my side, Margaret, and tell me if we are a suitable couple, in outward aspect at any rate.

MARGARET. Oh ! if you want to get rid of me, say so at once, I won't stand in your way, though I don't suppose the law would separate us because you choose to wear old clothes and to stoop. Now do go ; the people will be coming. [*Exit* SIR HENRY.]

MARGARET. Thank goodness it's nearly over; I am tired of worrying him. How kind and good he was, and so patient—for he must think it's only a fad of mine. As for the absurd nonsense he talks about himself, I can't make it out. Perhaps he thinks I want to turn into a frisky matron, and so he reminds me that I must be staid as becomes the wife of a would-be Methuselah [*laughs*]. No, bless him. he knows better than that; besides, he's too guileless to suspect; it's nothing but laziness—an excuse to wear his old clothes. Of one thing I'm certain—he would be furious if anybody took him at his word and treated him as he pretends to treat himself, and this article will make him frantic, but I think it may cure him of his mania, only, poor dear, I hope it won't hurt his feelings; luckily it's too palpably absurd for that, all the more if I improve upon the original, which I've a good mind to do. The stronger the dose the quicker the cure. I wish I could cure him also of that ridiculous habit of speaking of me as if I was a baby [*catching sight of herself in the glass as she walks about*]; small blame to him though, when I dress in this foolish way. Really this frock with its baby sash is only fit for a child of five years old . . . and this thing [*taking up the hat*], it's like a doll's hat, any man might look like my grandfather when I'm turned out like this—I wonder it never struck me before . . . [*After thinking for a minute she makes a sudden gesture and flies out of the room, slamming the door after her.*]

[*Enter* SIR HENRY—*then* ROONEY.]

SIR H. [*comes in dressed in frock coat, grey trousers, his hair cut, moustache trimmed, and looking twenty years younger; walks about*]. Margaret! Margaret! where the deuce are you? After giving me all this trouble, and making me look like a fool, you might at least wait and tell me what it's all about. She has got something in her head, I'll be bound, for she's so considerate, so careful never to run counter to any of my prejudices and lazy ways. I must be patient and trust her thoroughly—aye, and so I do, God bless her . . .

ROONEY [*running in with a pin-cushion under his arm, and brushing a hat as he comes to the front*]. Beg pardon, Gineral, but you nearly got the start of me. You were off, before I had half complated you. There's your honour's tie to be pinned down behind, just becos those she divils of laundresses, bad luck to 'em, pulverize every button they come across. Be jabers, if I don't think they swallows 'em. And what will her ladyship say! She tould me you was to be turned out as spick and span as a jeweller's shop, on a fair day.

SIR H. You're a deuced deal more anxious to please my lady than you are to please me, Rooney. —Now don't go on fiddling with my hat, put it down and do what you want with the tie, and then be off with you. I've had more than enough of this tomfoolery.

ROONEY. That may be, Gineral —but the day you was married to the iligant-est and best lady I ever clapt eyes on, you said, says you, "Now mind, Rooney, you'll obey her ladyship and do every mortal thing she tells you;" so now, Sir Henry, you'll plase sit down so as I can get at ye, and I'll put the finishing touch to ye in no time. We've been pretty smart about this 'ere dressing, too. [*He makes* SIR HENRY *sit down in an armchair and turn sideways.*]

SIR H. [*laughing*]. Smart; yes, indeed, and it's not the first time we've had to be smart about it. Do you remember, Rooney, that morning at Basfontaines, when those rascally Boers attacked the camp?

ROONEY. You may well say that, Gineral. I mind me it had just gone four in the morning when the alarm sounded, and by ten minutes past we was all in the saddle waiting for the Major, bless his ould heart, who couldn't find his boots at all, at all, in the dark of his bell tent.

SIR H. Short, sharp, and decisive, eh! Rooney? and when it was over, I, for one, was glad enough to get back to camp and tumble into bed again without your help. There [*he throws himself back in his chair*] that'll do—you've had your way and bothered me enough in all conscience. Now go and tell her ladyship, that if she does not come at once, I'll go back to my room and put on my old clothes again. What the deuce can she be doing with herself!

ROONEY. It's all right, Gineral. I heard her calling out for Susan as I come along, and they're as busy as bees, I warrant. You can't catch them idling their time at all, at all.

SIR H. Be off with you, and give Lady Milman my message, instead of talking—

ROONEY. I'm going, Gineral. [*He goes towards the door, aside*] The darlint—she'll come fast enough when she knows the Gineral wants her . . . heart alive, what's this! [ROONEY *meets* MARGARET *at the door and starts back, uttering an exclamation. She silences him with a gesture, and he goes out muttering*] Well, I never did—this bates cock-fighting—whatever has she been and done to herself!

[*Exit* ROONEY.]

[*Enter* MARGARET.]

MARGARET [*comes in behind him on tip toe and puts her hands over the back of his chair, concealing herself from him. She is beautifully dressed in a very becoming costume, but one suitable to a married woman of thirty years old. She peers over and examines him*]. Well, the captain's quite satisfied now. You do look handsome; have you inspected yourself? for if so, you will be quite conceited enough, without my saying anything.

SIR H. Not I. I had enough of that when I saw myself by your side just now. But having done my part, now for yours, and for the third time, what's the meaning of it all?

MARGARET [*while she hesitated he looks round, trying to see her*]. First you must promise—a real promise, mind—to sit still, as quiet as a mouse, and not to move till I give you leave . . . promise.

SIR H. Yes, yes; go on.

MARGARET. A horrid newspaper [*she begins quietly, but gets excited as she goes on*] says the most insolent things . . . talks of you —(of course the man only saw you at the station), as being old and stooping and looking at least seventy. Now be quiet, you promised . . . [*All this time* SIR HENRY *is struggling to get up, and swears under his breath while she holds him down.*]

SIR H. The devil he does? I'll show him.

MARGARET [*she goes on very quickly*]. And he talks of me, and says that you'll repent of your temerity, and insinuates . . .

SIR H. [*at last bounding up in a towering rage*]. Brrrrr—! The scoundrel! I'll break every bone in his body . . . He shall see to his cost if I'm an old man, and to say that *you* . . . The devil of it is, though, that I can't take the law into my own hands in my position here, but I'll prosecute him, I will. I'm an old man of seventy, am I? and decrepit—am I? And what did you say he insinuates about you, Margaret? Have I brought this upon you in addition?

MARGARET. If you will only sit down quietly for two minutes more [*she keeps dodging behind so that he shouldn't see her*] . . . I'll show you a better way to punish him than breaking his bones, which you must not do, or prosecuting, which you shall not do. We'll make his famous article the laugh of the county. And now the murder's out, I want to show you to them to-day—as you are now—and myself, as I am, and I flatter myself that (*throwing her arms about and speaking theatrically*], it will puzzle them to find a handsomer couple.

SIR H. [*who has subsided on his chair and speaks in a subdued, sad tone*]. Ah, my darling, you've made a mistake there. It is the showing us together that you should avoid, if you want to confute that rascal. There's the mischief. For myself alone—well, I think I'm passable, in spite of my fifty odd years, and could hold my own with some of them yet. [*He straightens himself in his chair.*] But seeing me with you is where the shoe pinches. They have a right to call me an old fool—though not, thank God, to insinuate that . . .

MARGARET. But why will you always talk as if I was a child ?

SIR H. Merely because you look so young; for in intellect—in charm of conversation—in all that constitutes a perfect woman, few, if any, could compare with my Margaret, but the other side of the question is also true. Alas ! this morning when I came in from my ride, it struck me more forcibly than ever. . . . I give you my word that, seeing you for the first time, any one would have said you were a girl in the schoolroom.

MARGARET. Oh ! thank you ; I'm extremely obliged—very flattering, indeed—an insignificant school girl. A bread and butter miss, of all things the most vapid and stupid. Thank you ; and did you happen to look at my gown ? Was it suitable and becoming to the little girl who wore it ? or didn't you even observe it ?

SIR H. I never observe much what you have got on, as I am always looking at yourself—and thinking you the loveliest and most loveable of all the . . .

MARGARET [*interrupting and laughing*]. Children you ever saw ; isn't that it ? But about the gown, do try and remember.

SIR H. I remember it perfectly ; it was a muslin frock.

MARGARET [*majestically*]. What *women* wear are called gowns.

SIR H. Yes ; but it didn't look like a woman's gown, I remember thinking it a sort of baby get-up, but it became you, as everything does.

MARGARET. Well, now we'll go back to our editor [*he begins to explode again*]. If you were to break his bones, you would only be taking up the quarrel of somebody else ; of some old, decrepit man who had married a girl of fifteen . . . What a goose he must have been—there I quite agree with the editor. And now, if you please, we will forget him for a time, and show to the assembled rank and fashion of this ancient town the handsome couple I spoke of—a perfectly well-assorted and exceedingly beautiful pair ! [*He had got up when she again alluded to the article, and she had been gradually pushing him before her towards the mirror. When they reach it, she suddenly comes forward and puts herself by his side.*] Let me present you to General Sir Henry Milman,

a decrepit old gentleman of seventy, and to his baby-wife of fifteen years old.

SIR H. [*starts back in unfeigned amazement ; seems unable to speak for a minute or two. Then he takes her hand, and with his other hand furtively brushes away a tear*]. Margaret, Margaret, what have you done ? I thought I could never love any one better than my childlike wife. But another has come between us and taken her place, one who makes me unfaithful to that earliest love ; one who is from henceforth the all-perfect woman in my eyes. The loveliest ! the dearest ! the . . .

MARGARET [*affected too, but carrying it off with a radiant smile*].
Hush, hush! [*as the doors are thrown open*] perhaps it's the editor
himself; here comes the advanced guard of our first "At Home" [*as a
servant announces* COL. *and* MRS. SINCLAIR, CAPTAIN *and* MRS.
GRANT], and I think everybody will admit that we are—"Well
Matched after all."

Curtain slowly falls as SIR HENRY *and his wife advance to meet
their guests.*

ALTERNATIVE PART FROM PAGE 59.

MARGARET—PETER.

MARGARET. Have you got all the General's things ready, as I told you ? and varnished his boots ? and, above all, Peter, don't forget to cut his hair a little, and do make him wax his moustaches !

PETER. Aye, aye, my lady ! But I expect the General 'll wax himself into a towering rage ! He don't like to be put about—he don't ; and I don't think he'll like all this neither [*pointing round the room*].

MARGARET. Nonsense, Peter. Sir Henry always likes what I like. And as to putting himself in a rage ! how dare you say so, Peter ! The General's never angry ; or if he is, other people are sure to be in fault.

PETER. Umph !

MARGARET [*laughing*]. Now don't go on with your everlasting Umph ! [*imitating him*], but listen to me. You love your master, and you're proud of him, or you ought to be—aren't you, Peter ?

PETER. Proud of him ! Aye, my lady—aren't he one to be proud of ?

MARGARET.—And I'm proud of him, and I mean every one to know it, and they shall, too, with your help. But, dear old Peter [*coaxingly*], though you and I think there's no one so handsome and grand-looking—still, when people see him for the first time in those very odd-looking clothes—you know, that old jacket, and those hideous trousers !

PETER. Aye, aye ! . . . They went through three cam—

MARGARET [*interrupting him*]. Oh ! yes, I know ; I know ; and I love the old rags. But they're not exactly becoming ; and, somehow, he's got a way of stooping when he wears them ; and then he lets his hair grow all shaggy. In short [*suddenly exploding*] . . . Now, look at this, Peter; there's an insolent newspaper [*taking it out of her pocket and pointing to it*] which calls him an old man, and jeers at him for having married a young wife, and dares to insinuate that I . . . Oh! it's too shameful!

PETER. The devil take 'em! I ax your pardon, my lady, for swearing; but, old as I am, I'd like to get hold of that 'ere scoundrel as wrote it, and I'd give him such a basting as he wouldn't soon forget! I'd print something on his ugly face—that I would!

MARGARET [*laughing*]. That I'm sure you would, Peter. But I've thought of a better plan still—to turn the laugh against them all, and to set every one talking of the handsome Sir Henry Milman, and of what an enviable woman his wife must be . . . Won't that be splendid? [*rubbing her hands with delight*]. So now you'll help me, won't you, Peter? You know the General lets you do what you like. Why, I've heard him say you're the best barber in England; and that means that you're as good a barber as you're a faithful servant . . . Dear old Peter!

PETER. There you are, my lady, coming soft sawder over the old man. There's no resisting you.

MARGARET. That's right, Peter; of course you won't go against me, because all I'm doing—you well know—is for your dear master's sake. But I think I hear him riding into the stable-yard. Just help me to get these flower-baskets out of the way, and push some of the chairs back. The General has a way of rushing in in a tremendous hurry, and then he stumbles over everything. [*They arrange the furniture.*] [*Aside*] I'm in an awful fright, but I don't mean to let him see it, not I. [*Aloud*] Now run away, Peter, and get all his things ready.   [*Exit* PETER.]

ALTERNATIVE PART FROM PAGE 69.

PETER [*running in with a pin-cushion under his arm, and brushing a hat as he comes to the front*]. I ax your pardon, Sir Henry, but you went off before I. had half finished you. There's your tie has got to be pinned down behind all along o' those laundry women who rip off every mortal button they come across. I'm blest if I don't think they eat 'em, and what will her ladyship say! She told me to turn you out as smart as a new pin, General.

SIR H. You're a deuced deal more anxious to please my lady than you are to please me, Peter.—Now don't go on fiddling with my hat, put it down and do what you want with the tie, and then be off with you. I've had more than enough of this tomfoolery.

PETER. That's likely enough, Sir Henry, but you must please to remember that the day you married her ladyship, bless her heart, you'll excuse an old man for saying so, General—you said, says you, "Now mind, Peter, you're to obey Lady Milman in every single thing she orders," so now, Sir Henry, I'm going to obey her, and so must you. If you'll sit down, I'll finish you up properly in no time. We've been pretty smart about it as it is. [*He makes* SIR HENRY *sit down in an armchair and turn sideways.*]

SIR H. [*laughing*]. Smart; yes, indeed, and it's not the first time we've had to be smart about it. Do you remember, Peter, that morning at Basfontaines, when those rascally Boers attacked the camp?

PETER. You may well say that, Sir Henry. I remember, it had just gone four in the morning when the alarm sounded, and by ten minutes past there we was in the saddle and waiting for the Major. He couldn't find his boots all along of its being so dark in his bell tent.

SIR H. Short, sharp, and decisive, eh! Peter? and when it was over, I, for one, was glad enough to get back to camp and tumble into bed again without your help. There [*he throws himself back in his chair*], that'll do—you've had your way and bothered me enough in all conscience. Now go and tell her ladyship, that if she does not come at once, I'll go back to my room and put on my old clothes again. What the deuce can she be doing with herself?

PETER. It's all right, Sir Henry. My lady was calling out for Susan just now, and as I come along I could hear 'em bustling about in her ladyship's room. They're always busy about something—never idle they aren't.

SIR H. Be off with you and give Lady Milman my message, instead of talking—

PETER. I'm going, I'm going. [*He goes towards the door, aside.*] Aye, aye, my lady'll come soon enough, looking so purty and smart—she never keeps the General waiting she don't. Bless me, what's all this! [PETER *meets* MARGARET *at the door and starts back uttering an exclamation. She silences him with a gesture, and he goes out muttering*] Well, if this don't beat cock-fighting. Whatever has she been about! [*Exit* PETER.]

BRIC-A-BRAC.

Characters.

MRS. SPOONER . . *Widow of the captain of a merchant vessel.*

SIGNOR LUCCA ROBBIA
(otherwise Mr. Luke } *An æsthetic character and collector.*
Robbins)

MARTHA . . . *Parlour-maid.*

SCENE *laid in a seaport town—a common-place room, but filled with all · sorts of curiosities—ivory, carved wood, china monsters, &c.*

MRS. SPOONER [*very smartly and vulgarly dressed for a garden party. Speaking to some one outside through the door.*] You understood, Martha, didn't you? A fly at three o'clock . . . it's now half-past two, just time for a thorough overhaul, as poor dear Spooner used to say. [*Looks in the glass.*] Steady, not so bad after all, though I had to follow Cousin Julia's orders about my dress for this fine party of hers, the first she has given since her wedding; handsome but simple, she said . . . not to scare her new family. They're prim folks, I suppose. So I've taken in a reef or two. Never mind, I make a very tolerable figure even so, and if my poor dear had seen me in this get up he would have been as proud as Punch of my tautness . . . How proud he was too of his collection, as he called it! For my part I thought most of it rubbish. During all his voyages cases and cases used to pour in till the house looked like a pawnbroker's shop. Ugly old nodding monsters and

china dishes with slimy-loooking creatures crawling over them . . .
Now, if he'd brought a nice new dessert service with plenty of gold on
a bright pink ground, as we had at home before I married, I'd have
said. thank'ye. However, he was a good husband, was my poor
Spooner, and it's a cruel fate to be left a widow in one's prime. [*Looks
out of window.*] Rain, rain, and a horrid sea fog. I can't help thinking
of that comical-looking man, with great goggle eyes, though he was
handsomer, I must say, than dear Spooner. Who can he be? He
has been following me about like my shadow for some days, and I
shouldn't wonder if he has fallen in love with me at first sight, as they
say. If he came prowling about here to-day, what a drenching he
would get, and how I should laugh—it would cool his ardour a bit.
[*Some one knocks at the door.*] . . . Well? what is it?

[*Enter* PARLOUR-MAID.]

MRS. S.   I said a fly at three o'clock.

PARLOUR-MAID.   I beg your pardon, mum, but a gentleman has
called and begs to see you on very pressing business.

MRS. S.   I told you I wouldn't see anybody . . .

P. MAID.   And that's what I told him, mum, but the gentleman
insisted on my bringing up his card.   [*Gives card.*]

MRS. S.   Signor Lucca Robbia, I never heard of such a name
[*pauses*] . . . Yes, now I come to think of it, Spooner used to read
about that man in the papers [*reflects*]. Oh! I know; he goes about
collecting what they call break-a-back, pick-a-back, or some such
outlandish name . . . but what on earth can he have to say to me?
[*looking at the card*].   "Urgent business."   [*Turning to the servant.*]
Show him up.   [*Exit* MARTHA.]   [*Sits and reflects.*]   Why, I never
asked her what the man was like! what a droll visit to be sure . . .
and what can I have in common with a foreigner who buys old broken
furniture, and bits of china at auctions . . . Now if poor Spooner
was alive . . .

[*Enter* SIGNOR LUCCA ROBBIA.]

MRS. SPOONER [*aside*]. Gracious me, the man with the goggle eyes! This passes a joke. [*Aloud, with indignation*] Sir, may I beg you to explain?

SIGNOR LUCCA ROBBIA [*aside*]. She has evidently recognized me. [*Aloud*] For heaven's sake, Mrs. Spooner . . .

MRS. S. I must request you to leave the room, sir, or you will oblige me to ring, and use forcible means to . . .

SIG. L. R. Pray, pray, madam, listen; only one word. In the name of all you hold most·dear, in the name of your collection itself, let me say one word . . . [*All this time* SIG. LUCCA ROBBIA *is looking around with irresistible curiosity, and furtively examining the ornaments, china, &c.*]

G

MRS. S. [*aside*]. The man's evidently mad, but he looks a gentleman, and is very well dressed. The fly's not come, Martha's within call, so for the fun of the thing I'll hear what he's got to say for himself.

[*Aloud*] Well, Mr. Robbia, since you have got into my house, I'm willing to listen, so speak out and explain.

SIG. L. R. Indeed, Mrs. Spooner, I can but give you the faintest outline of the terrible position in which I find myself . . . the merest sketch.

MRS. S. [*pointing to a chair*]. You'd better, at any rate, sit down.

SIG. L. R. [*bowing and sitting down*]. In a word, madam, I am the unfortunate man, the despairing wanderer, who has dogged your footsteps persistently during the last few days ; alas, I fear that you are prepossessed against me, but let me assure you—

MRS. S. [*coldly*]. Come to the point if you please.

SIG. L. R. In spite of the disdain which you evince towards the most respectful of interrogators, believe me, madam, that the motive which brings me here is profoundly legitimate and correct.

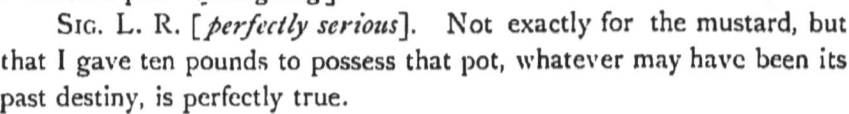

MRS. S. [*bridling up*]. I should hope so, indeed . . . I know all about you ; you are a crockery fancier, a collector of break-a-back and curios, and Captain Spooner told me that you once gave ten pounds for a mustard pot. [*Laughing*].

SIG. L. R. [*perfectly serious*]. Not exactly for the mustard, but that I gave ten pounds to possess that pot, whatever may have been its past destiny, is perfectly true.

Mrs. S. I must once more beg you to tell me what you've come for.

Sig. L. R. Then, madam, I proceed to tear aside the veil—

Mrs. S. [*impatiently*]. Tear it, then, but be quick about it, please.

Sig. L. R. Imagine then, madam, a beautiful afternoon—no, it was pouring cats and dogs, I remember; I had gone to a broker's where a private collection was being sold. I was bidding for a superb soup tureen, an unexceptionable specimen of old Chelsea. Gold anchor nearly two hundred years old. Ah! that was a tureen! The flowers and foliage with which it was decorated, would have rejoiced the heart of

 William Beckford himself. In addition, a very rare occurrence, it was enriched with magnificent armorial bearings. Ah! madam, I had dreamt, longed inexpressibly to be the owner of such a treasure . . .

Mrs. S. [*aside*]. Mad as a hatter. [*Aloud*] This *Chelsea 1745* joke has been carried far enough.

Sig. L. R. [*eagerly*]. Joke, madam, I'm as serious as Pluto himself, but I'll condense. This tureen, then, was awarded me for thirty-six pounds fifteen shillings and ninepence—I'll spare you the farthings.

Mrs. S. Thank'ye for that.

Sig. L. R. [*in an agonized voice*]. Alas! alas! Mrs. Spooner, this tureen—the dream of my youth, the ideal of my riper years, this unparalleled tureen had been deprived of its cover!

Mrs. S. [*drily*]. Sorry for you, Mr. Robbia, but I can't help you, and if—as I suspect—all this is done for a bet, made at my expense, you may consider that you've lost it, and had better go. [*Points to the door.*]

Sig. L. R. Cruel, cruel, can you send me away thus?

Mrs. S. [*angry*].   Bless the man !   I've not got your cover.

Sig. L. R.   Inconceivable delusion !

Mrs. R.   What do you mean ?

Sig. L. R. [*speaking rapidly and with excitement*].   Do not attempt to deny it, for I know all.   The missing cover is here, in this very house, and . . . [*reproachfully*] you use it to hold a lamp in your greenhouse.   Ah ! we collectors—we votaries of the beautiful, the antique, we cannot be deceived.   My friend, Vandyke Brown—I mean my friend Vandyke, saw this very cover, this precious lid, in a curiosity shop at Seville ; it was bought by the captain of an English merchant ship, and addressed with other objects of rare art to some house in this town, but he had forgotten the name and address. Fast as the express could bring me I came—I searched—I inquired— all in vain.   When sitting on day sipping a glass of lemonade—one cannot eat when the heart is heavy within one's breast—the pastry- cook's young man exclaimed, " There goes the young widder as has got all the fine things, why her house is like a pawnbroker's shop, they comes home by the score in the merchant ships " . . . I darted out in pursuit of you, but for a week past, often as I caught sight of you, you evaded me !   At last I find you.

Mrs. S.   This is lunacy, Mr. Robbia.

Sig. L. R. [*with violence*].   Ah, you think so because you are not a collector, you know nothing of that devouring passion.   When we are seeking the object of our desire, we track the enemy as does the wily Indian, eager to scalp, and proud to nail the trophy at the door of his wigwam.   And I had sworn to obtain your cover.   Oh, Mrs. Spooner . . . conceive a soup tureen without its cover.   It is the solitary palm tree sighing at the northern blast.   It is Paul separated from his Virginia.   A Siamese twin torn from his fellow.   For the love of heaven, Mrs. Spooner, sell me this priceless cover. [*Kneels at her feet.*]

Mrs. S. [*recoiling aside*].   I'm   really   frightened. [*Aloud.*]

Wait one moment, Mr. Robbia. [*She rings.* MARTHA *appears.*] Bring me that ornamented tureen cover, it's in the greenhouse . . . [*Exit* SERVANT.]

SIG. L. R. What, madam, is it possible that you really consent?

MRS. S. To give up the cover? Certainly.

SIG. L. R. [*ecstatically*]. Certainly! Exquisite adverb! I know not how to express my gratitude. But let me ask you the price you put upon this precious morsel?

MRS. S. No price at all, I give it you with pleasure. [*Aside*] Too glad to get rid of you anyhow.

SIG. L. R. [*with sudden suspicion*]. You give it me—Chelsea! marked with the gold crown. Then—oh heavens! —then the enamel must be injured or—some secret defect . . .

MRS. S. No, it's all right [*a noise is heard as of china falling down and breaking*] at least it was just now. . . . Mercy, what's that? I'm—afraid—I'm very much afraid, Mr. Robbia . . .

SIG. L. R. Heavens! What's that I hear? Oh, what a mortal blow. . . . My—your—our cover—Mrs. Spooner, I feel faint—I—I —Chelsea with the gold crown—I . . . smashed in a thousand pieces! Ah! Ah! [*Sinks down fainting.*]

MRS. S. [*stupefied, and aghast*]. My word, here's a set out. . . . Mr.

Robbia, Mr. Robbia; oh, he has fainted as he threatened. What an awkward position! [*Distracted*] I beg you to recover. He don't move, it's awful. If he was to die. . . . Signor Robbia, in mercy to me—a corpse in my house and at this hour! [*She loses her head*] Not one spare room in this miserable little place. Oh, it's horrible . . . Suppose I try slapping his hands. [*She slaps them*] Do come to, there's a dear man. . . . There's the party, too, what will become of me? I can't undo his collar. Oh! if my poor Spooner was but here in this crisis. . . .

[*He moves.*] Ah! he's recovering—I'm saved!

Sig. L. R. Where am I? Ah, Mrs. Spooner, is it you? What has happened? [*Opening his eyes.*] Ah! I remember —the co—ver . . . [*Goes off again.*]

Mrs. S. [*beside herself*]. Oh, don't go off again, there's a good creature!

Sig. L. R. [*again recovering*]. It's over now—I feel better—I have—to—thank you—

Mrs. S. [*anxiously*]. Now are you really better? Shall I get you a glass of water?

Sig. L. R. Yes, with sugar, if you please. [*She runs to a sideboard and gets it.*] [*He looks with disdain at the glass she brings him.*] Bah! sham Venetian . . . [*Drinks.*] There, there, I am perfectly —mended—thorough restoration—I know not how to apologize—but the truth is that my nervous system has become completely demoralized —ever since—

Mrs. S. [*curiously*]. Ever since?

Sig. L. R. Since the breaking off of a marriage which promised to ensure my perfect felicity.

Mrs. S. I'm very sorry I'm sure.

Sig. L. R. [*sitting down*]. Your kindness emboldens me. Oh! Mrs. Spooner, suffer me to confide in you, it would solace me to tell you some details of my private—my miserable private history.

Mrs. S. [*aside*]. The man's impudent if he isn't mad—I must really—and this party . . . [*Aloud*]. Mr. Robbia, I'm really very sorry, but I'm already late; I'm going to a party—you can see by my dress.

Sig. L. R. Two words will suffice for the simple facts—a few years ago my parents—

Mrs. S. I'm sorry, but really you mustn't go on, I can't stop any longer, it's a sort of wedding party—

Sig. L. R. [*interrupting*]. Ah! heavens, it is of a wedding that I am speaking—of my own wedding, which did not take place because the young girl who was—ripening—if one may use the figure—trained in the parental hothouse—till I could claim her—in fact, Miss Griggs—

Mrs. S. [*aside*]. Griggs! [*Aloud*] Did you speak of a Miss Griggs?

Sig. L. R. [*sentimentally*]. Yes, madam, it was that young lady whom I was to wed—my seconds—our parents I mean, had arranged the affair, but ere I could lay at the feet of my betrothed, who was the ornament of her county—the expression of my devotion, this dear but volatile young person had bestowed her precious hand on another, a man engaged in the mercantile navy, I believe.

Mrs. S. [*aside*]. Mercantile! Griggs! an extraordinary coincidence! [*Aloud*] I'm very sorry for you, Mr. Robbia, but really I can't—[*breaking off*]—This is a very curious name of yours, is it really your own?

Sig. L. R. No, dear madam, not exactly, it is an improvement, a—recollection; and keeps ever before me that of one, whose name is a household word to all true lovers of the beautiful, the sublime. My

own name, that of my parents, is alas! supremely vulgar, and mingled
with the happiness I felt on first seeing my beloved idol, was the pain
I endured at hearing her name—so fatally prosaic. Oh! what a
hideous fate! . . . That two souls knit together by the sublimity of
ethereal passion—one soul I should say, since my love was unrequited,
—should be chained to earth amid sordid surroundings—our place of
meeting a race ball—our names Luke Robbins and Matilda Griggs!
. . . [*All this time passing his hands through his hair, speaking incoherently and gesticulating wildly, he stands the picture of despair.*]

MRS. S. [*aside*]. Mercy on us! Matilda Griggs! no longer a
doubt . . . so this is the man, the rival of my poor Spooner . . . My
parents thought he was mad, when he rushed into their room the day

after that ball, and went down on his
knees to be allowed to marry me.
They wouldn't even let me see him.
[*Aloud*] Then I suppose, Mr. Robbia,
I'll still call you so as you prefer it,
though for my part I like honest English
names best, I suppose you are very
angry with the poor young girl, but it wasn't her fault.

SIG. L. R. Angry! No such unworthy feeling blends with the
sacred remembrance of my Matilda, yet you will readily believe that
this refusal, for no apparent cause, was a crushing blow. She did not
know me, and I had only once seen her; nevertheless I had built up on
this union a host of happy conceits. Ah! it was a terrible awakening
. . . That, Mrs. Spooner, was the reason why I threw myself into
ceramics in the zenith of my youth.

MRS. S. [*aside*]. My poor Spooner himself could not have re-
gretted me more. . . . [*Aloud*] What do you say? Ceramics! what
are ceramics?

SIG. L. R. [*confused and vehement and not noticing what she said.*]
Yes, Mrs. Spooner, up to my eyes in ceramics; at any rate, in acting

thus, for I wished to preserve a profound respect for the sex of which Miss Matilda Griggs was, in my eyes (it was before I had the honour of meeting you), the one perfect specimen ; at any rate, as I said, in acting thus I have never been tempted to say of woman, what Hamlet thought. No ! in my days of profoundest discouragement I had only to exclaim : Frailty, thy name is—china.

Mrs. S.   And you are a bachelor still for *my* [*catching herself up*] —for *her* sake ?

Sig. L. R.   As was the Shepherd Paris, madam.

Mrs. S. [*aside*].   What in the world is he talking about ? there are no shepherds in Paris that I ever heard of . . . [*Aloud*] Forgive me if I seem to be prying into secrets, but have you never come across Miss Griggs since that time ?

Sig. L. R.   Never.   The gentleman she preferred to me, was the captain of a merchant ship, and his name, let me think—is—is—Fork, something I think like Fork or Forker.

Mrs. S. [*laughing*].   No ! more like Spoon : his name was Spooner !

Sig. L. R. [*absently*].   Ah ! perhaps then I should have said that Spooner was the name of this ruffian sailor.

Mrs. S. [*with violence*] . . . Mr. Robbia, respect, if you please, the memory of my husband.

Sig. L. R.   The memory of—your—husband !   Spooner your husband . . . [*Suddenly enlightened.*] . . . And—you are now . . . a—widow—and—and—then is it ?—oh ! can it be . . . Miss Matilda Griggs whom I have the overpowering felicity of addressing at this moment ?

Mrs. S. [*aside*].   Well, the murder's out now, and there is no good in denying it.   [*Aloud, with dignity*]—Sir, it is to the widow of Captain Spooner that you addressed yourself for the purchase of—the cover.

Sig. L. R. [*in frenzy of delight*].   Oh ! marvels of the ceramic art ! all is now explained.

MRS. S.   All explained—what can you mean, Luke?

SIG. L. R. [*sentimentally*].   Luke! you call me Luke? Ah! Mrs. Spooner, even that plebeian name from your dear lips becomes glorified.   This is worth years of suffering.   Yes! all is explained! whilst I believed I was only pursuing with ardour that golden-crowned treasure which at this instant is lying close to us, smashed in a thousand fragments; night and day I was persistently following on your track. Ah! Mrs. Spooner, the tenderest sentiments were gradually awakening towards you in my heart. And, after all these days of vain research, it was no longer the cover of a soup tureen that I sought, it was yourself, the being whom I adore.

MRS. S. [*coquettishly hiding her face with her hands*]. La! Mr. Robbia.

SIG. L. R. [*distractedly*].   I bitterly reproached myself for my disloyalty to the sacred memory of Miss Griggs, and if the collector had not upheld the courage of the lover, neither one nor the other would have had the happiness of prostrating themselves at your feet, as they now do, beseeching you to bestow—

MRS. S. [*turning her head aside*]. Oh, Mr. Robbia.

SIG. L. R. [*very agitated and confused*]. Oh, pardon my audacity, and as the result of this strange adventure, oh! Mrs. Spooner, deign to complete my collection! Ah! forgive me, I am losing my head, deign, I mean, to recompense my long-enduring constancy,—one word will efface the memory of all my sorrow; with tears of emotion, my beloved one, I

entreat you to have pity and to grant me your cover! Oh! I must be mad—to grant me—your hand!

MRS. S. Well, then, considering the dreadful smash of your poor tureen cover through Martha's stupidity, I suppose I must make what amends I can to the unfortunate collector!

SIG. L. R. Away with all thoughts of the tureen; what care I now for the rarest porcelain? I love you—and you alone.

MRS. S. [*simpering*]. Really, Mr. Robbia— your unusual constancy does deserve a reward, but after all [*puts her handkerchief to her eyes*] what am I? [*Sentimentally*] Only a sorrowful widow— with not much of a heart to give. . . . Like the poor cover, my heart has been broken.

SIG. L. R. [*excitedly*]. Ah! let me mend it—with cement and strong tapes.

MRS. S. My broken heart?

SIG. L. R. No, no, the cover! Heavens, I don't know what I'm saying.

MRS. S. [*laughing*]. You do seem all abroad, I must say—and this dream you talk of is smashed. What is it worth to you now?

SIG. L. R. [*with transport*]. I will be its consoler.

MRS. S. [*laughing*]. The consoler of my cover?

SIG. L. R.   No, my Matilda, but of your heart—the pieces are still complete.

MRS. S.   The pieces of my heart?

SIG. L. R. [*distractedly*].   Oh, for heaven's sake let us have done with these horrid misconceptions—darkness melts away, daylight appears.   The soup tureen vanishes : you remain, and I adore you.

MRS. S.   Even without my cover?

SIG. L. R.   With all my tureen!   Ah!   [*A knock at the door.*]   [*Enter* SERVANT.

MRS. S.   What is it ?

SERVANT.   The ornamented cover which you asked for, mum, has just been found in the cupboard.

MRS. S.   Then what was the noise I heard just now ?

SERVANT.   A flower stand upset by the dog, mum ; and I came to say the fly is just driving up.   [*Exit.*]

MRS. S.   Well now, Luke or Robbia ; I get so bothered with all your names, what do you say now ?   The cover is not broken after all.

SIG. L. R.   I deeply regret it, for you will now dismiss us both for ever `. . . the cover and my unhappy self—my unhappy self and the cover—and I shall certainly fall a victim to my undying love . . .

MRS. S.   No, Luke, I shan't dismiss you for ever, or the cover either—only just now I must send you away.   To-morrow we'll discuss these serious matters—now I must be off to the first party given by my friend Julia Doughty, a cousin of my poor dear Spooner's.

SIG. L. R.   Miss Julia Doughty who has just married *my* friend Robert Graves ?

MRS. S.   Yes.

SIG. L. R.   That being so, I will beg for a place in your carriage [*takes note out of his pocket.*]   That note, this costume [*pointing to his smart clothes*], indicate that I too am going to a party, and it is to the one given by my friend Graves and his bride.

Mrs. S. Another happy coincidence. Do you then know Mr. Graves intimately ?

Sig. L. R. Intimately—y-e-s—I may say so—for we crossed together from Dover to Calais and were both very sick. Those are the experiences that bind people together for life. Then, too, he collects bric-a-brac—his wife will be a happy woman.

Mrs. S. As to that, we shall see, meantime I'll give you the place you asked for just now, but it's a fly, not my carriage. Bless you —I don't keep a carriage. Come, Luke, and —about the cover, what orders am I to give ?

Sig. L. R. Desire them to place it on the sideboard of your dining-room—and perhaps some day my soup tureen may come to rejoin it, if you will give your consent.

Mrs. S. Luke Robbins, you have it, and with it my whole collection of—what's the word ?—break-a-back.

CURTAIN.

TIT FOR TAT.

~~~~~~~

Characters.

LORD EDWARD CHERITON.
BLANCHE, *his wife.* ·
A SERVANT.

SCENE:—*A man's sitting-room. Armchairs, sofa, cigar-cases, pipes, a litter of pamphlets, sporting papers, &c.*

[LORD EDWARD *discovered asleep in armchair.*]

[*Enter* SERVANT *bringing in morning papers.*]

SERV. Asleep; I'll take precious good care not to wake him, or shouldn't I catch it!   [*Puts down papers, and exit on tip-toe.*]

LORD E. [*talking in his sleep*]. Now then, looking-glass next, and then masks! [*Hums a valse.*] One more turn before the— [*moves his legs as in dancing and throws down tongs with a clatter*]. Hulloa! what's the matter? [*rubbing his eyes*]. Why, I thought I was still at—and here I am in my own room—twelve o'clock. By jingo, I've been asleep above an hour! What will Blanche think of me? But I got up so early—no, I mean I went to bed so late—I feel all nohow; that comes of making a fool of one's self, and at my age too, seeing that I'm over thirty-five, and adore my wife. . . What an idiot I am! But there it is, I cannot help it. As I say, I adore my wife, and I feel a brute for leaving her so much alone; but a man must have some sort of amusement, and goodness knows mine's innocent enough, just a cotillon or two, a few dinners, and a supper now and then. It's such a nuisance that I'm always forced to tell her a parcel of white lies. Darling Blanche! I'm awfully fond of her, but perhaps she's a turn too strait-laced. Earnest is the word nowadays. She thinks a man

ought to pass his life, when he's not at home, at the House, or on committees, or doing something useful. As to society, balls, and that sort of thing, she thinks it awfully frivolous. A fellow don't like his wife to think him frivolous, especially when he adores her, and so I'm driven, as I said, to deceit, which is beastly. Dear little Blanche! She don't understand things. If I told her I was going to dine at Greenwich, I verily believe she'd think I was going to dine with the old pensioners [*pauses*]. The fact is, I married her before she could have come across any other fellow. She had never been out in London, and is a perfect child in the ways of this wicked world, and she looks up to me as a paragon of virtue. It's rather exhausting to have to keep up that reputation. One has to be posted up in the debates too. Luckily, it's easy enough to get up a smattering about the army and navy, which all the fellows talk so much about [*yawns*]. Heigho! [*pauses*]. Well, there was last night—I told Blanche I was to help get a scientific swell into the Travellers', and that there'd be a late House, and she wasn't to sit up. She swallowed it all!—asked no questions, and I felt a brute. Of course I did mean to go for the balloting, but I couldn't resist a jolly dinner at Greenwich that Mrs. Churnley got up in a hurry, and then they all wanted to sup at the Skiffington, and afterwards there was this infernal ball. I swore I would not stay for the cotillon, for I'm sure to make an ass of myself; but Mrs. Churnley had no partner. So there I was, don't you know. Dash it all, it's rather Blanche's own fault after all! Why does she shut herself up? If she would come to Greenwich—No—no—I don't think it would suit her—N—o—o [*drawling*]. I shouldn't like her to belong to that set exactly, but if she cared for—dancing—just dancing . . . as I do—what could be the harm?—and we should be together. I never flirt, or that sort of thing. One has one's pals of course—and so might Blanche. Eh! no—no—. I shouldn't like that either, for I don't approve of married women having pals. I mean, of course, one's own wife; other fellows must look after theirs; but as to Blanche—I should be furious; and as to flirting, she wouldn't know what it meant —dear little unsophisticated thing [*yawns*]. Oh bother—how difficult it is to square it all round [*pauses*]. Blanche has only got one weakness—diamonds and jewels in general—so I've made a little system of compensation which I can confidently recommend to all husbands who are devoted to their wives, but who are also devoted to flir—I mean cotillons.

[*Enter* SERVANT.]

SERV. A parcel, my lord—from Skirrum's.

H

LORD E.   Oh, I know.   Give it me; the man needn't wait.

SERV. [*gives parcel*].   The bill's enclosed, my lord.

LORD E.   All right [*looking at the bill*].   Well, that's a facer; but I deserve it [*pauses*].   This is my system, whenever I stay out late and make a fool of myself, and tell these confounded lies, which is what I hate doing—only what can a man do who adores his wife, and don't like to annoy her? . . . Well then I punish myself and please her. As I said before, she has a weakness for jewels, so I give her the best I can afford; and, by Jove, don't it walk into the money!   If the season goes on much longer, I shall have to put down my hunters [*sits down and opens the case*].   Well, this is a stunner, pearl and diamond hoop.   If Blanche loves one thing more than another it's a good ring.

[*Enter* BLANCHE.]

BLANCHE.   Am I disturbing you?

LORD E. [*quickly shutting up the case*].   Of course not, dear—as if you ever could, you little goose!

BLANCHE [*who saw what he did, aside*].   Just as I thought. . . . Now for it.   [*Aloud, but coldly*]   Anything in the papers?

LORD E.   No—but what's the matter, Blanche?

BLANCHE.   Nothing that I know of.

LORD E.   For a moment I thought . . . of course I was mistaken. How are you, dear, this morning?

BLANCHE.   Perfectly well, thanks—and you?

LORD E.   Me—oh, I'm all right.

BLANCHE [*looking at him*].   You look rather tired.

LORD E.   Tired--oh, no—at least, I was rather late.   Blanche, have you quite forgiven?

BLANCHE [*pretending astonishment*].   Forgiven—who and what?

LORD E.   Me, dear.

BLANCHE [*same by-play*].   What for?

LORD E. For leaving you again last night . . . I left you to dine alone.

BLANCHE [*interrupting him and sitting down*]. So you did ; I'd quite forgotten.

LORD E. [*nettled*]. Forgotten, had you ?

BLANCHE. Yes, because just before dinner—

LORD E. [*hastily interrupting and piqued*]. Oh, never mind why you forgot my absence . . .

BLANCHE [*cheerfully*]. Well, did you get your man in ?

LORD E. What man ? Where ? [*crossly*].

BLANCHE. That distinguished scientific swell you were anxious to get into the Travellers'. Our memories seem both rather at fault this morning.

LORD E. Oh, ah !—why, yes—yes—of course. But now about you, Blanche, what did you do with yourself? I thought so much of you, all alone.

BLANCHE. I ? Oh, I worked and read, and I went to bed soon after eleven, and just—

LORD E. [*interrupting her*]. Dear, good Blanchie. [*Aside*] And at that hour I was at the supper—before the ball—I really am ashamed of myself. [*He gets up and leans over the back of her chair, holding the jewel-case behind him.*] [*Aloud*] Do you know what I was thinking of just now as I looked at you ?

BLANCHE. I suppose I can guess.

LORD E. What was it ?

BLANCHE [*indifferently*]. That I looked lovely.

LORD E. No . . . at least, of course I thought that too, but it was much more.

BLANCHE [*as he hesitates*]. Well ?

LORD E. . . . I was thinking how wrong it is to leave you so much alone.

BLANCHE [*interrupting*]. But if I don't mind being left ?

LORD E. Ah, but you are so good and patient—that's what makes me ashamed of myself.

BLANCHE. I can't see the necessity for such excessive remorse.

LORD E. [*aside*]. But I. do. [*Aloud*] Well then, Blanchie, to prove to me that you quite forgive—will you make me happy by—[*he hesitates*].

BLANCHE [*calmly, as she goes on working*]. Accepting this little present ?

LORD E. Yes ; that it makes me so happy—

BLANCHE [*same by-play*]. To give you—

LORD E. Just so—but how did you guess ? [*Looks uncomfortable, suspicious.*]

BLANCHE. Because you're so generous and—so—often—make me presents.

LORD E. That's all bosh about generosity ; but, Blanche—you won't refuse to take this, will you ? [*Caressingly.*]

BLANCHE. Refuse . . . why should I ? You've already given me—let me see—two brooches, three pair of earrings, five rings, and as many bracelets, quite lately, and why should I refuse this particular one ? [*Looks up at him.*] . . . What is it this time ?

LORD E. A ring ; pearl and diamond hoop. I think you delight in pearls, don't you ?

BLANCHE. I think you might feel sure of it by this time [*looking at the ring*]. It's lovely ; thanks so much. But there's one condition I make—in accepting—

LORD E. Of course—any condition you like.

BLANCHE. You must let me do as much for you.

LORD E. [*recoiling, astonished*]. Eh ?

BLANCHE. I have got my little present for you, also.

LORD E. For me ?—but why ?

BLANCHE. But why not ? Why do you give me presents ?

LORD E. [*aside*]. Confound it ! what does she mean ? [*Aloud*]

Because — because — naturally, you know, it gives me im-mense pleasure.

BLANCHE.   Then it's not fair to deprive me of the same im-mense pleasure.   I've noticed that your purse, though inexhaustible as to its contents, is getting very old — so I got this one for you [*pulling a purse out of her pocket*].   I hope you'll like it, dear.

LORD E. [*declining to take it*].   Thanks; but—[*aside*] I don't like this at all.

BLANCHE [*holding out the purse*].   There—give yours with the left hand, and here's mine with the right—exchange is no robbery, you know. Well ! [*as he shows no intention of taking the purse.*] Doesn't that suit you ?

LORD E. Perfectly. [*Aside*] Not the least in the world. However, what must be, must. [*Very unwillingly takes the purse and gives the jewel-case.*]

BLANCHE [*looking at the ring*]. What a beauty !

LORD E. [*looking at the purse, but speaking coldly*]. Charming. [*Turning to his wife.*] A thousand thanks—but—you must not make me any more presents.

BLANCHE. I'm sorry you don't like the purse.

LORD E. I like it enormously . . . it's not that . . . [*Aside*] What the devil's come over Blanche ? I never knew her the least like this before.

BLANCHE. Then it's very selfish to want me to give up the enormous pleasure— Do you remember, the other day you showed me in Skirrum's window—a lovely set of studs ? You admired them so much.

LORD E. I daresay—I don't remember.

BLANCHE. I found those were sold, so I ordered another set for you. They were promised me for this morning—I'm expecting them now.

LORD E. [*much agitated*]. No, Blanche, that's impossible ; I can't allow— [*Aside*] What the deuce does all this mean ?

BLANCHE [*cool and unconcerned, but pretending astonishment*]. You can't allow ?

LORD E. There can be no sort of reason why you should give me expensive presents. [*He walks up and down in an agitated manner.*]

BLANCHE [*innocently*]. But those you give me are even more expensive.

LORD E. Quite a different thing. I don't choose you to waste your money.

BLANCHE. But you waste yours.

LORD E. I tell you that it's entirely different. A husband may surely give presents to his wife.

BLANCHE. And not a wife to her husband?

LORD E. Certain'y not, for the same rea—I mean not in the same way. What—a purse, and an expensive set of studs . . . it's absurd; and all in one day!

BLANCHE [*insisting*]. Then you refuse?

LORD E. Distinctly.

BLANCHE. But [*coaxingly*] if I ask it as a favour?

LORD E. I refuse all the same.

BLANCHE [*throwing herself into an armchair with an air of absolute indifference*]. Oh, well, if it's on principle, I've nothing more to say. [*Takes up paper, and pretends to read, watching her husband furtively*].

LORD E. [*aside*]. If it's on principle? Can she mean anything by that? What a devil of a fix I'm in. Blanche can't have any motive for suddenly following my example about presents. No, no; impossible. Does she suspect that I sometimes deceive her as to my whereabouts, for that's really all—or nearly all. Could she have heard about little Mrs. Hoppingham? For though there's nothing to hear, still, in these days one can't speak to a woman without some idiot chaffing about it. If I could but find out, but it's working in the dark, and I might put something into her head, something which, of course, doesn't exist. What an infernal set of gossiping mischief-mongers one does get mixed up with! why can't people mind their own business, and leave other people alone? Hang it all, and I who adore my wife! [*going to Blanche, aloud*] Blanche, darling!

BLANCHE [*pretends to be absorbed in her paper and doesn't look round, but holds out the purse*]. Here it is.

LORD E. [*coaxingly*]. Listen to me, Blanchie.

BLANCHE [*repeats mechanically*]. Here it is.

LORD E. No, no; a thousand times, no. [*Walks up and down in an agitated state, then pauses*]. You seem wonderfully engrossed with that paper.

BLANCHE. Yes; it's very terrible [*reads out*], " It is feared that a fresh disturbance on the north-west frontier is imminent, General Roberts is advancing." [*Sighs deeply.*] Poor Charles!

LORD E. [*uneasy*]. What makes you so keen about Gen. Roberts' movements, and who do you mean by Charles?

BLANCHE. Why, Charley Redmond, my cousin. I think you saw him once.

LORD E. [*brightening*]. In the Scarlet Lancers, isn't he? quartered in India, aren't they?

BLANCHE. Yes, but Charles is in England now, you know.

LORD E. How the devil should I know? Have you seen him, pray?

BLANCHE. Of course I have, several times, and he came here just as you went out yesterday. I was telling you when you interrupted me.

LORD E. You were doing nothing of the sort, and you had no business to receive him without telling me. What an odd time to come!

BLANCHE. Perhaps he thought he was sure of finding you at home at seven o'clock. [*Aside*] I scored one there!

Lord E.   Oh! and what did this beloved cousin say for himself?

Blanche.   Not much; he is a great deal too modest to talk of his own deeds, but he's got the C.B.

Lord E. [*interrupting*].   As if every fellow didn't get that now-a-days.

Blanche [*going on in the same tone*].   And the V.C., that, I believe, is *not* given to every fellow.

Lord E.   There's a deuced deal of luck even in that, I'm told. [*Aside*] Surely this infernal cousin can't have anything to do with Blanche's sudden freak of giving me presents?

Blanche [*returning to her paper*].   If this news is true he will be obliged to go back at once.   Oh! [*in a low tone of voice and sighing deeply*] poor dear Charley!

Lord E.   What does a fellow go into the army for, pray, if he don't want to fight?

Blanche.   He does want to fight, but, naturally, poor fellow, to return so soon, when he—when we—had just renewed our old friendship. Oh, I can't bear to think of what may happen to him.

Lord E.   Then don't think about him.

Blanche.   Not think about Charley? when we were brought up together.   At one time there was [*sighs*] even a question of—but it couldn't be.

Lord E.   What a pity.

Blanche.   Thanks, you're too kind.

Lord E.   Come now, Blanche, let's be serious about these studs.

Blanche [*getting up*].   Ah, then you've come to your senses. They'll be here directly.

Lord E.   No, no; but do tell me the truth, dearest.   Is it, that— [*Aside*] Hang it all, I must find out somehow . . . And yet it's putting things into her head whatever I say . . . [*Hesitates.*]

Blanche.   Well?

LORD E.   Perhaps you've heard something, and you want me to understand that—

BLANCHE.   Heard something, and want you to understand ? [*Eagerly*]   Oh, do tell me what you mean.   You know how curious I am ; and I'm dying to know.   Anything that interests you ?

LORD E. [*aside*].   I can't make her out.   [*Aloud, with temper*] No.

BLANCHE.   That worries you ?

LORD E.   No.

BLANCHE.   That would interest me, then ?

LORD E. [*getting more savage*]   Not in the least.   [*Aside*] I'm d—d if I can make out what's come to her.

BLANCHE.   I'm just dying of curiosity, and you must tell me what you mean.

LORD E. [*exasperated, pulling his moustaches, but trying to seem indifferent*].   Nothing, nothing.   I don't even remember what I was going to say.   I was thinking of something else.

BLANCHE [*looking fixedly at him*].   You seem very absent this morning, and you look ill.   Is anything the matter ?

LORD E.   No, no ; don't worry.   [*Aside*] Evidently I shan't get anything out of her.

[*Enter* SERVANT.]

SERV.   A parcel just come for your ladyship.

BLANCHE.   Who from ?

SERV.   From Skirrum's, the jeweller, my lady.   [*Gives her the parcel*].

BLANCHE [*advances towards her husband, holding the parcel high up*].   Here are the studs.

LORD E. [*speaking sternly*].   I have said, once for all, No.

BLANCHE [*opening the case*].   Pearls, like my ring ; don't you care for pearls ?

LORD E. [*folding his arms*].   No.

BLANCHE [*cheerfully*]. That's very disappointing. You know they're from the same place, Skirrum's; and [*reproachfully*] you admired them in his window. [*Pause*] So, you decline them?

LORD E. [*with arms folded and looking away from her*]. Yes.

BLANCHE. You'll regret your decision; for if you had taken them I would have told you—

LORD E. [*eagerly*]. What?

BLANCHE. All you wish to know [*maliciously enjoying his discomfiture*].

LORD E. You would have told me why you wish to give me these studs?

BLANCHE. Just so.

LORD E. Is that true?

BLANCHE. You had better find out by . . .

LORD E. By?

BLANCHE. Accepting.

LORD E. Very well. Tell me first, and then . . .

BLANCHE. No conditions! Take them—or—leave them.

LORD E. [*aside*]. She's pitiless. [*Aloud*] Blanche, you've got the obstinacy of a man.

BLANCHE. And you, my dear, the curiosity of a woman. Now then—one—two—

LORD E. Three. I accept, since so it must be [*sighing*].

BLANCHE. At last.

SERV. [*throws open the door*]. Luncheon is served.

BLANCHE. What a blessing! I'm dying of hunger.

LORD E. But your promise?

BLANCHE. After luncheon.

LORD E. [*determined*]. No, Blanche; I won't stand this sort of thing any longer. You promised, and I hold you to your promise.

BLANCHE. I submit, since so it must be [*imitating him sighing*]. But we had better put off luncheon; conjugal explanations take time.

LORD E.   Never mind luncheon ; go on.

BLANCHE [*evidently trying to put off the evil moment*].   Well, then, you wish to know ?

LORD E.   Why you gave me the purse and studs ?

BLANCHE.   [*She nerves herself and speaks slowly and with difficulty at first, then gets more animated.*]   Well, then, to begin at the beginning.   We've been married five years. [*Pauses, looking furtively at him.*]   For the first three or four you often made me little presents, trifling in themselves, but valuable to me, because they were your gifts, and proved that I was often in your thoughts.   But, when latterly it came to jewels, valuable diamonds, it was another thing . . . and after a time an odd idea took possession of me.   I thought of those Madonnas in the Italian churches, covered with votive offerings.   It was explained to us, don't you remember ?— they were given either in a moment of repentance, or as an expiation.   I couldn't help connecting those two ideas, and wondering—I even began to think that I understood the motive—

LORD E. [*interrupting*].   Granted, for argument's sake—but what on earth has that to do with your presents to me ?

BLANCHE [*coquettishly, but laughing to herself all the time*].   Oh, if you can't put two and two together—there's such a thing, Edward—as—tit—for—tat.

LORD E. [*jumping up in a fury*].   Blanche ! you dare—you stand there and dare to tell me, your husband—that—you have deceived me ?

BLANCHE [*clapping her hands*].   Caught—caught ! so that's what tit for tat would mean, is it ?   I might have doubted before—now you've shown yourself up with a vengeance.

LORD E. [*he walks up and down, trying to calm himself, and then comes and stands before her with his arms folded and speaks gravely*].   Now look here, Blanche, supposing that I have lived in rather a fast set, gone to suppers, balls, and stayed out late—kept perhaps by a stupid cotillon, when you thought I was at the House, you may certainly call it deceiving—but can you compare that sort of deception with your own—about this cousin—never telling me he was in England, that you were expecting him last night, and—and—in short am I to understand that you were engaged to him, and that you deceived me at the time of our marriage ? . . . If that's a fact—I can never again believe in any human being—

BLANCHE [*aside*]. I think I have teased him nearly enough, poor dear. [*Aloud, putting on a serious air.*] Now that you have confessed what I have suspected for some time—and have discovered that I'm not such a simpleton as you suppose, I have a confession to make to you on my side, Edward—about my cousin [*pretending to be confused and shy*]. It's painful to me to admit that I have deceived you. [*Movement of Lord E.*] But you won't be too hard on me, you must promise to forgive . . . [*This must be comic.*]

LORD E. [*furious, aside*]. To think that a woman with the face of an angel—a saint as I believed her to be—could be so black-hearted—could stoop to deceit [*looks round at* BLANCHE, *who has her face hidden in her hands to conceal her laughter*]. But, poor child, she seems heart-broken, and I hate to see her miserable—though she deserves it—and I who adore her, and never cared two buttons for all the Mrs. Hoppinghams in creation. . . . [*Aloud*] Speak, Blanche, you're torturing me—forgive you ! yes, no doubt I shall be weak enough to forgive *you*, but as for that scoundrel—that black—

BLANCHE [*interrupting*]. Oh, don't be hard on him, Edward—it's not his fault, at any rate. [*She comes to him and lays her hand on his shoulder ; he wants to shake her off, but looks at her and relents.*] The truth is—that—to the best of my belief—my cousin—Charles Redmond —has never—left—India—since he went there six years ago. . . . [*She makes a comic face.*]

LORD E. [*aghast, not knowing what to believe*]. You mean that he did not—that you did not—that after I went out—he—

BLANCHE. I mean that—when you left me, yesterday, I saw the children put to bed, then I dined—read—worked—and thought of you at the Travellers'!!

LORD E. [*still bewildered, and passing his hand over his forehead*]. What a confounded ass I was—to fancy for one moment that you . . . Blanche . . . [*brightening up*] you're an angel [*going to her and taking her hands*] . . . do forgive me, dearest.

BLANCHE [*drawing her hands away, but still half-laughing*]. Not so fast, please . . . I'm an angel . . . of course—but about yourself, Edward ? The votive offerings and expiations ?

LORD E. Stuff and nonsense about votive offerings and expiations . . . as if I ever gave a thought to any one but you—

BLANCHE [*again interrupting*]. Oh, come ! come !

LORD E. [*going on*]. As if they mightn't all go to the deuce for what I care, Mrs. Hop—

BLANCHE [*laughing*]. Stop, stop, English law, you know, don't allow people to criminate themselves—no names, please.

LORD E. Why not ? Gossiping idiots do couple names for no earthly reason, and you may have heard them. Blanche, you can't really mean—you never could doubt me in that sense, or believe that, with all my folly, I ever wronged you by a thought.

BLANCHE [*gravely*]. No, Edward, if such an idea had ever crossed my mind—should I have made a joke of it ?

LORD E. But then what does all this mean ? Let us at any rate have it all out now, and begin on the square.

BLANCHE [*seriously*]. It means that latterly we have been drifting apart, and—it's not in your nature, Edward, to—fib, and you don't do it at all well—and so—

LORD E. Ah—that *has* been the hateful part. I was disgusted with myself—but I didn't like you to despise me—and you are rather down on frivolity, as you call it, aren't you, Blanche ?

BLANCHE. Well, perhaps I will admit there are faults on both sides—and we ought mutually to . . . [*pauses*]. Now suppose I take to going out more with you . . .

LORD E. [*eagerly*]. Then I'll stay at home more with *you*—but just one word, Blanche ; there never was a question of an engagement between you and Redmond ?

BLANCHE [*laughing*]. That's not fair—bygones—you know the proverb—[*looking up at him mischievously*]—let us invent a system of compen—sa—tion . . . [*he winces*] . . . As to the past—my cousin against cotillons—as to the present—

LORD E. [*interrupts*]. As to the present—perfect confidence, and for the future—

BLANCHE [*pulling out her watch*]. For the future, among other things, cold luncheons, unless we're more punctual. [*Takes his arm.*]

[*Exeunt, arm-in-arm.*]

CURTAIN.

CROCODILE TEARS.

Characters.

LAURA, *Romantic Widow of Colonel Edgar Kennedy.*
BEATRICE, *her Sister.*
Scene, a small sitting-room—door at the back opening to garden—arm-chairs, tables, &c.—a dog's basket.

[*Enter* LAURA *and* BEATRICE *together, quarrelling.*]

BEATRICE.   There's an end of it, Laura.   I'm worn out; nothing shall induce me to go on like this.

LAURA.   To hear you, any one might think I was the tyrant; instead of which it's you, who worry me to death.

BEATRICE.   Then you'll be glad to hear that you need no longer be victimized, for I've made up my mind to go away.   If you choose to shut yourself up in this absurd manner, it's your affair.   But I can't stand it any longer; it acts on my nerves.   Our view of nature is bounded by the garden wall, and our view of humanity by our own faces.

LAURA.   How cruel of you to taunt me !   You, who know what I suffer [*puts her pockethandkerchief to her eyes*].   Have you no sympathy for your poor sister, left a desolate widow ?

BEATRICE.   Pshaw !   You needn't remain desolate if you don't like it.   You chose to make an absurd resolution—

LAURA.   A good resolution can't be absurd.

I

BEATRICE.   An absurd resolution can't be good.   However, that's not the question.   I don't want you to marry.   I only say that with plenty of money and good looks you may put an end to the widowhood you complain of whenever you please.·

LAURA.   It's not the widowhood—as you unfeelingly call it—that makes me miserable ; but the loss of my beloved husband.   You've no sympathy, Beatrice : not a grain of it.   My poor dear colonel was the best and kindest of men.   [*Weeps.*]

BEATRICE.   Who should know that better than myself?   But Edgar hated exaggeration, and would have strongly objected to all this sentiment; your best affections wasted on a dog.   At any rate, while he was with us, Laura, you didn't appreciate his presence as much as you appear to regret his absence.

LAURA.   I loved him with all my heart! [*aside*] I'm sure I did, in spite of—[*hesitates*].

BEATRICE [*aside*].   Then your heart had an odd way of showing it.

LAURA.   He adored me.   He lived and died for his country and for me.

BEATRICE.   He lived to do his duty.   As for dying, no doubt he would have died for his country if it had been necessary.   No doubt, too, if you had tumbled into the river, he'd have jumped in after you ; but, as a matter of fact, poor dear Edgar died of—liver·—

LAURA.   Heartless girl !   Perhaps you would insinuate that he died from eating too much.

BEATRICE.   I insinuate nothing.   He liked a good dinner when he could get it ; but you weren't famous for looking after his comfort in those matters ; and now he's gone, you show no respect for his memory by these perpetual waterworks.   He wanted you to lead a useful life ; it should make him turn in his grave to see you idling it away—not an interest, not an occupation, but·—feeding that wretched dog.

LAURA.   So you want me to part with my dog—the only remaining tie . . . linking me with former happy days !   ·

BEATRICE. Nonsense! I want you to be reasonable. You've taken into your head to play the part of an inconsolable widow. But I'm not a widow, and don't mean to sacrifice myself any longer. Do get rid of this bee in your bonnet—about eternal regrets—[*aside*]—eternal fiddlesticks!

LAURA. I see what you're at; you want to drive me to marry again. I consider that a woman degrades herself by replacing the beloved object of her first affection. Still, if you insist—for your sake, for that alone, mind—I might try to overcome my repugnance.

BEATRICE. Oh, pray don't think of such a thing for my sake! indeed, I shouldn't care to live with a woman who degrades herself. But why can't we be jolly—see something of the world—of society?

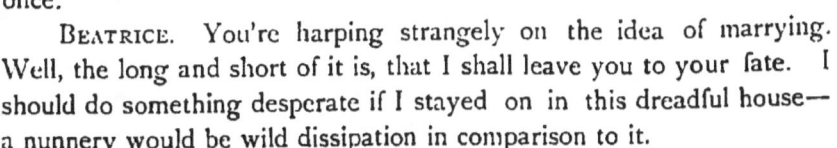

LAURA. Oh, no; if it's necessary to be gay, better marry at once.

BEATRICE. You're harping strangely on the idea of marrying. Well, the long and short of it is, that I shall leave you to your fate. I should do something desperate if I stayed on in this dreadful house—a nunnery would be wild dissipation in comparison to it.

LAURA [*with asperity*]. Perhaps *you* may be looking out for a husband.

BEATRICE. Not I. You've given me no chance since poor

Edgar's death. The gardener's the only man I see, and if he wasn't so old I should feel shy of speaking to him. As to the curate, I've got so unaccustomed to anything wearing a coat that I positively blush when I meet him. No! I'm all for liberty; and thanks to the importation of American ideas, one gets a fair share of it nowadays. I speak in your interest; if you choose to be obstinate, so be it, only don't dignify it by the name of constancy.

LAURA. I beg you'll allow me to be the judge of my own actions. One would think you were the elder of the two.

BEATRICE [*sarcastically*]. One would indeed!

LAURA. I've said my last word.

BEATRICE. And a very foolish one it is. [*Walks to the end of the room, collecting things as if for packing.*]

LAURA [*aside*]. What a position I'm in! I should like to confide in Beatrice, but having so often scoffed at the idea of marrying, I couldn't own myself beaten; besides, the memory of my vow haunts me. [*A dog is heard barking.*] Ah! there's my precious Bijou calling me. I daresay they forgot to give him his rissole. [*Exit* LAURA.]

BEATRICE [*coming back to the front*]. Oh, that dog! It exasperates me. I lose patience, temper, heart—all the virtues one's supposed to possess; and when I think of what Edgar suffered with Laura's caprices and follies, not to mention the way she neglected him, this pretended affliction provokes me past all endurance. How surprised he would have been if he could have foreseen the line she takes; he was afraid she wouldn't give a decent time to her weeds. It's absurd, considering I'm two years younger, the way poor Edgar left her in charge to me; but there's a limit to everything, and I'm come to the end of my tether. And yet perhaps I may be driven to matrimony myself; but at least I won't be a humbug, or pretend it's to please any one but myself. But would it please me? Aye, there's the rub! I expect to hear from Arthur soon. . . . I told him I couldn't give an answer for at least six months, and the time's nearly come now. The fact is, I hate the thoughts of giving up my liberty. How I envy the servants! If they don't like a place they can leave it, and they certainly do, when it suits them, without the smallest scruple. But in families it's supposed that we must all be tied together. I've the advantage of being independent, and it makes me feel rather lonely at times [*pause*] But to return to Laura. I can't make her out—I really can't. She didn't care for Edgar; she married him out of pique—that was clear enough. But it was not so clear why Captain Sedley went off without proposing to her. His ship was certainly ordered off to the West Indies, but that didn't deprive him of the use of his tongue, or at least of his pen; however, off he went—Laura married Edgar, worried his life out while he lived, has worried mine out since he died, and now makes the very house damp with these eternal tears, and what for? For the loss of a man she never cared for? or because Captain Sedley hasn't shown signs of life? I've my suspicions. He must be coming home soon, and Laura has been more restless lately. . . . Can she have had a letter? She's very close, and having taken up this idiotic line she'd be ashamed to own it, if she has changed her mind. I must contrive a plan to circumvent her. It is funny that my Arthur should have joined her Alexander's ship at Bermuda, and be serving under him. Funnier still that their initials should be the same, A. S. S.—Arthur Stephen Swan, Alexander Sloan Sedley. I think I can make something out of it. Hush! here she comes, and with that horrid dog of course.

[*Enter* LAURA.]

LAURA. Poor little fellow! Has he lost his master? Where is his master, darling? Ah! he's left us for ever, my pet. ‘Bijou’ will never see him again.

BEATRICE. Unless he goes to join him.

LAURA. What did you say? Beatrice, you're a brute.

BEATRICE.   What's the matter now ?

LAURA.   You've a heart hard as the nether millstone.   You've no feeling for the woes of other people.   You don't even understand them. You're ungrateful to the memory of the kindest, the dearest [*weeps*].

BEATRICE [*aside*].   The waterworks turned on again.   I shall go mad.   [*Aloud*]   That's not true.   I remember dear Edgar with the utmost gratitude, and I show my respect for his memory by doing all that I know he would have wished. [*Aside*] Oh ! dear, I'm sorry she reminded me of him just now when I'm going to leave her ; for I can't pretend that he would have wished that.

LAURA [*continues without heeding her*]. You laugh at my grief, you hate the very dog who loves me. Poor pet, he too has lost all his gaiety since his master went, haven't you, my pet [*weeps again*].

BEATRICE.   Laugh at you !   I wish I could laugh at anything ; but I've lost the power of laughing.   I'm very nearly as melancholy as you are yourself.

LAURA.   As if that were possible.

BEATRICE.   It's not difficult, I assure you, under the circumstances. And as to ' Bijou ' I do my best to love him—

LAURA [*interrupting*].   Oh ! oh !

BEATRICE [*speaking to the dog*]   Don't I, dear ? [*teasing the dog*]. Now, my sweet pet [*imitating her sister*]. make a bow.   Now a little valse.   [*Aside*]   Oh ! the little brute.

LAURA [*trying to seem indifferent*].   Beatrice, what's the weather like ?   Do look out and tell me if it's going to rain !

BEATRICE. Rain? why, it never stops raining. The very sky seems to be widowed.

LAURA [*sighing deeply and carrying the dog, kissing him. Walks to the window and looks out*]. Darling pet.

BEATRICE. Well, I shall go now and write to auntie. I shall say I'll be with her this day week.

LAURA. Oh! why put it off so long? Why not go at once? So far from wishing you to remain, I shall rejoice to feel you are happy.

BEATRICE [*aside*]. Ah! there's something in the wind. Hitherto whenever I've broached the subject of leaving her there's been a cataract—Falls of Niagara—I thought the house would be swamped in her tears. Now she seems in earnest. I shall soon see. I'll try the weeping line myself. [*Aloud*] Very well, Laura; so let it be. I'll put my things up and come back to say good-bye; and, perhaps, when I'm gone . . . you'll think with more kindness of the poor sister who has devoted herself to you all these years [*puts her handkerchief to her eyes*] and who loves you so dearly. [*Aside*] That'll bring her round, I think. I never knew her lose an opportunity of mingling her tears, as she calls it.

LAURA. I shall always love you, dearest; but as my sorrows disturb your life, and deprive you of the gaiety natural to your age . . . it *is* better that we should part.

BEATRICE [*recovering and speaking briskly*]. It's a pity you hadn't thought about my gaiety a little earlier. However, if that's your line, the sooner the better. [*Aside*] When she sees I'm in earnest she may yet change her tone. [*Aloud*] I shall telegraph at once, and go off to-night, since you're so anxious to get rid of me.

LAURA. If you make haste John can take the telegram before he brings up luncheon.

BEATRICE [*aside*]. No, no, my dear; you've shown me your cards, and now I'm going to play out my own little game. [*Aloud*] All right, I'm going out now, but shall be back to luncheon. [*Exit* BEATRICE.]

LAURA. Was ever woman in such a dreadful position? Sometimes I feel to be a thorough hypocrite; yet it is not hypocrisy, for I
mourned most truly for my poor dear Edgar. Ah! perhaps I did not
appreciate him as he deserved while he was with me, and in the agony
of my grief and remorse I registered a vow to devote the rest of my life
to his memory. For a long time I banished every other thought; but,
alas! for the weakness of human nature. When I went last year to
visit one of Edgar's relations I met my—my fate! Ever since that
time I have been torn by conflicting emotions and wishes—constancy
to the dead, devotion to the living. How can I admit that I have
fallen from my own ideal? Yet how can I relinquish the heaven
opening to me in the possession of Alexander's love? I am tormented,
too, with doubts and jealousies. In the struggles I made to be true to
my vow I tried to conceal my feelings from Alexander, and though I
consented to see him again in a year's time, I gave him little hope, and
begged him to consider himself free . . . Six months later I learnt
that he had met Beatrice at our aunt's country house. From that time
I have known no peace. What if in his anguish he should have
turned to another for consolation? I dare not question Beatrice.
Nor is she likely to confide in me. Alas! wrapped up in my own
selfish emotions, I have never tried to win her confidence. I console
myself with thinking that if Alexander had cared for her he would not
have gone off to a distance—the other day my aunt mentioned him in
the most indifferent way. " Your friend, Alexander Sloane Sedley,"
she said, " has taken himself off to Bermuda." And I ask myself, is he
wiling away the time until he may again approach me, or has Beatrice
banished him? A few days must solve this dreadful doubt. Meantime, how thankful I am at Beatrice's determination to go away. I
must have time for reflection —my poor Edgar! Can I set aside your
cherished memory? [*After a pause.*] Alas! alas! Alexander, shall
I have strength to relinquish your precious love? [*weeps*]. I hear
Beatrice. I must conceal my relief at the prospect of her departure.

[*Enter* BEATRICE, *with hand-bag, cloak, strap, packages, &c*]

BEATRICE. There, I'm all ready; but I must wait for the eight o'clock train instead of going at three o'clock as I intended.

LAURA [*with her back turned, and pretending to be occupied writing a letter*]. Well, dear, it's very sad to part, but in your interest I can't wish it otherwise ; and—last moments are so trying. Why do you put it off till eight o'clock ?

BEATRICE [*watching her sister closely*]. On account of a letter I'm expecting. A very important one—that may affect my—future life.

LAURA [*curious but otherwise indifferent*]. Your future life ? At all events, your letter can't now come till to-morrow morning. The second post came in an hour ago, so I can forward it.

BEATRICE. Yes. But the letter that I'm expecting wouldn't come by the second post. There's a third one that brings—

LAURA [*hastily interrupting her*]. No, the third post only brings letters from the Colonies—ship letters.

BEATRICE. How can you possibly know, since you can't get ship letters ?

LAURA. Why can't I, pray ?

BEATRICE. Why ? You, an inconsolable widow ! It's out of the question. A letter from out there could only be from an officer in some regiment, or [*watching her closely*] an officer of the fleet. [*Aside*] How odd ! She don't rise. But I mean to find out. Something's in the wind, and I shall lead her a pretty dance till I know. I've made a nice little plan, and luckily I can trust Susan thoroughly to carry it out [*goes to the window*]. Here he comes [*goes to the door and calls out excitedly*]. Susan, the postman has gone round to the back door ; fly and see if there's a letter for me.

LAURA [*walking about in an agony*] [*aside*]. What can it mean ! Beatrice can know no one out there except Alexander. Oh ! it can't be possible ! There *can* be nothing between them ! I daren't ask, it would show me up. Oh ! oh ! [*bursts into a flood of tears*].

BEATRICE [*aside*]. Waterworks again. Well, it must be kill or cure this time. If my suspicions are right she'll show herself up, and

I'll take care that it shall be cure. But if I've wronged her, then I shan't have the heart to go away, and that's decidedly kill. [SUSAN *is heard outside*]. A foreign letter for you, Miss. [BEATRICE *rushes to the door, gets a letter, and comes back, waving it in* LAURA'S *sight*]. Come, now, Laura, admit that you're dying of curiosity ?

LAURA [*twisting her handkerchief and trying to hide her anxiety*]. I suppose I may wish to hear—to know—of anything which concerns my sister, without being accused of curiosity [*sobs from time to time*].

BEATRICE [*aside*]. Poor thing, it's rather a shame to tease her, but it's all for her good, as our governess used to say when she did anything particularly disagreeable. [*Aloud, holding the letter behind her.*] Now, then, guess who it's from. I'll give you three chances. [LAURA *doesn't speak.*] Do you give it up? Well, I'll help you. Locality, Bermuda ; initials, A. S. S.

LAURA [*starts, and can hardly contain herself.*] Initials, A. S. S. ? [*throws herself on the sofa and speaks hysterically*]. Ah! perfidious wretch ! And you, my sister,—to wrest from me, a miserable being, alone in the world, the only stay—support. [*Throws aside her usual plaintive tone, and works herself up into a fury.*] Ungrateful girl ! Thrice perjured man ! After his oaths—his refusal to be set free !

BEATRICE. What in the world does this mean ! If he has been constant to you and that you care for him, why all this humbug ? However, though you don't deserve it, I'll be generous, and put you out of your misery . . . You forget that there may be other people in Bermuda, and that their initials may even be A. S. S., besides the object of your adoration. There, calm yourself, my letter is not from Captain Sedley.

LAURA [*in a fury of wrath and misery, and pronouncing the name with the utmost contempt*]. Captain Sedley ! as if I ever gave a thought to him. But tell me at once, who is that letter from? I insist upon knowing, Beatrice; I, your elder sister, who have the care of you, insist. [*Changing her tone.*] Oh! for pity's sake tell me.

BEATRICE [*who has remained transfixed with astonishment*] [*aside*]. What! another! Not even her old friend; and she must have been carrying on all this time, and kept me in the dark, and almost persuaded me to believe in her! Oh! I'll pay you off for all these miserable years . . . At any rate you shall pass a painful quarter of an hour. [*Aloud*] Well, you are a pretty example to your sister; and after having posed as a broken-hearted widow for three years, and having shed quarts, nay gallons, of crocodile tears, you now wish to pose as the guardian of my morals, do you? Thanks, all the same; I prefer taking care of myself. Laura, Laura, aren't you ashamed of yourself?

LAURA [*who has all this time been lying on the sofa with her face hidden, now rouses up, driven to bay*]. It's very well for you. You first steal the affection of the man I care for, and then you taunt me. [*Furiously*] When was it settled? how soon after he proposed to me? Miserable girl, at least let me hear the truth.

BEATRICE. You dare to talk of truth? Why, my hair stands on end at the bare recollection of the dreadful *fibs*—fibs, I say!—you've been telling me all this time! Now, on my side, I ask for the truth. Let me at any rate hear the name of the happy individual who has consoled you for the loss of the best—the dearest of men?

LAURA. Nothing shall induce me to tell you.

BEATRICE. It's very foolish of you. [*Aside*] I really can't help pitying her. Who knows? there might be a third A. S. S. [*Aloud*] Come, Laura, describe him.

LAURA. I won't.

BEATRICE. Well, answer my questions. Tall or short?

LAURA. Oh, Beatrice, be merciful!

BEATRICE. Not I. Tall or short? For the last time of asking: Tall—or—short?

LAURA. Tall? No. Oh! I don't know those miserable details.

BEATRICE. Dark or fair? Quick, quick! Dark or fair? [*Aside*] He seems to be neither. I'm beginning to get frightened. It can't be my youth by chance. Arthur, in fact, is nothing particular. [*Aloud*] Neither dark nor fair? Scarlet, then, of course?

LAURA. No—no!

BEATRICE [*aside*]. That's a comfort, for Arthur verges on carroty, and might, perhaps, be thought rather dumpy. I'm beginning to breathe. What next? Now then, Laura, the crucial question. The name? Get your wits together! Are you ready? Here's a smelling-bottle—strong salts.

LAURA [*hysterical*]. Oh, oh! Speak. No, no! don't speak. [*At this moment there comes a loud rap at the door.*]

BEATRICE. Stop, Laura. I hear voices downstairs. Do collect yourself. Let's be calm. [*Goes to the door and speaks to* JOHN *outside.*] What is it?

[*Enter* JOHN.]

JOHN. Two gentlemen are below, ma'am. This one asked for you, ma'am [*gives a card, the wrong one, to* LAURA], and this one for you, miss [*gives her the other card*].

[*Both, simultaneously.*]

LAURA [*disappointed*]. Lieutenant Arthur—Stephen—Swan.
BEATRICE [*equally disgusted*]. Captain Alexander—Sloane—Sedley.

[*After a moment's pause each seizes the card of the other.*]

[*Both* LAURA *and* BEATRICE *speak together.*]

LAURA.   My own Alexander!

BEATRICE.   My blessed Arthur!   Hurrah!   We've each got our own A. double S. after all!   But, Laura, what do you think of yourself now?

LAURA.   Be generous, and forgive me [*inclined to weep again*].

BEATRICE.   By all means; only for heaven's sake don't let's meet your future with crocodile tears!

CURTAIN.

www.ingramcontent.com/pod-product-compliance
Lightning Source LLC
Chambersburg PA
CBHW022336020726
47500CB00004B/1147